TL OAKMAN worked as a medical scientist and then in the field of public health for thirty-seven years before retiring in 2022. She lives in rural New South Wales and devotes her time to writing, travel, playing golf, and long lunches.

www.tloakman.com

RUN TILL YOU CAN'T

REVENGE IS MURDER

TL Oakman

First published 2025 by TL Oakman
www.tloakman.com

Produced by Independent Ink

Cover design by Catucci Design
Edited by Daina Lindeman
Internal design by Independent Ink
Typeset in Adobe Caslon Pro by Post Pre-press Group, Brisbane
Cover image: Romolo Tavani/istockphoto.com

A catalogue record for this book is available from the National Library of Australia

ISBN 978-1-7642361-0-2 (paperback)
ISBN 978-1-7642361-1-9 (epub)
ISBN 978-1-7642361-2-6 (kindle)

To my husband, my partner in life and love.

'Courage is not the absence of fear, but rather the judgment that something else is more important than fear.'

— AMBROSE REDMOON

PROLOGUE

A loud crack startled Cheryl Banes awake. Her head snapped up from the back of the couch, her eyes drawn to the front door as it flew open. She winced as the sudden movement made her head throb. The light streaming in from the doorway caused her to squint. The door hung open at an odd angle, still vibrating from being kicked. In the doorway stood two giants of men, looking like silhouettes with the bright sun behind them.

Cheryl tried to focus. Something was not right, but she couldn't get her mind to work. The Mary Jane she'd smoked for lunch and washed down with a bourbon slowed her mind. She'd fallen asleep sitting on her tattered lounge. In front of her, the ash from the remains of a cigarette sat in a foil pie case on the wooden box used as a coffee table. Her mouth felt dry. Without getting off the couch, she licked her lips and managed to wake up enough to swear at the men.

'Watcha fuckin' doing? Yar wrecked the door.'

The men moved toward her. With broad shoulders, bulging arms, and thick, heavy necks, they looked like the rugby players who drank at her local pub after a game.

A man mountain stood over her menacingly.

'Where is she?' he snarled.

'Where the fuck is who?' Cheryl spat back.

'Your bitch of a daughter.'

Cheryl laughed, which turned into a dry hacking cough.

'I dun know where she is. Wot she done?'

The man nodded to his mate, who walked through the lounge to the back of the house.

'Oi, watch ya doing? I tol' you she's not 'ere.' Cheryl pushed herself up and off the couch and stood glaring at the man.

'We're going to see for ourselves.' The man crossed his tree-trunk arms and stepped in front of her.

Cheryl didn't have the energy to put up a fight. She flopped back down onto the couch. These giants could do what they wanted. She was just pissed they'd broken her door. She licked her lips and eyed the empty bourbon glass on the box in front of her.

Moments later, the second man came back and shook his head.

'Tell her we'll be back.' The men glared at Cheryl, then turned and walked out the broken door.

Cheryl massaged her temples and rested her head back on the couch.

'Bloody cow. Now she's done it,' she muttered before dozing back into a welcome oblivion.

CHAPTER 1

Tory woke with a start. She sat up, her heart pounding in her chest. She glanced toward the bedside clock; the alarm would not go off for another ten minutes. Adrenaline coursed through her body.

What had woken her?

Through gaps in the curtains, early-morning fingers of sunlight invaded the room. Tory blinked in the half-light and looked at her husband, Brent, sleeping beside her. Unnerved, Tory felt a sense of vacancy, something odd in the air. She looked around the room, unable to pinpoint anything in particular. Nothing was obvious, but the unsettling feeling persisted. A sense the air around her had changed.

Tory inhaled and detected a hint of the spicy deodorant still lingering after Brent's shower last night. She looked around the room again. Nothing. Nerves on edge, she rolled out of bed, stepped over the cotton blanket kicked to the floor last night, and padded in bare feet to the other end of the house, where her beautiful daughter, Laura, slept. She stood in the doorway and looked in at her precious five-year-old curled up in the middle of her bed, the superhero coverlet tangled around her thin legs, her long blonde hair sticking out in all directions. Tory smiled. With her favourite superhero, Spider-Man, gripped in the crook of her arm, Laura looked peaceful.

Reassured Laura was fine, Tory looked at her watch. She should get ready for work. Tory walked back along the corridor, through the kitchen and dining room, past the lounge room, to their bedroom.

As she showered and dressed, the odd sense stayed with her. She gelled her short blonde hair to make sure it would stay spiked throughout the day. Her mind distracted, Tory applied her make-up and cursed as she realised the pink shade of lipstick just applied clashed with the red top and beige slacks she wore. She didn't see many customers at the air conditioning business, but Tory liked to look good. After a wonderful season of summer weekends and exercise, Tory was pleased with how fit and tanned she looked.

'Look good, feel good, work better' was her motto. She wiped off the offending lipstick and rummaged around in the cupboard under the sink to find a more suitable colour.

Get over yourself, she thought as she smoothed the lipstick onto her lips.

At this rate, despite waking early, she was going to be late. Tory knew they had a lot on at work today. Maybe she was just procrastinating to avoid work?

By the time Tory walked out of the bathroom, both Brent and Laura were at the kitchen table, eating breakfast. Thanks to Brent, Laura sat dressed in her school uniform, hair tamed into two braids and a bowl of cereal in front of her. Laura chatted away nonstop to her father about the day she had planned. While the scene in front of Tory was one of domestic bliss, she could still not shake her unease.

Brent looked up as she entered the kitchen and nodded in her direction.

'Morning, babe.'

Brent looked very sexy to Tory, dressed in his usual 'chippie' work gear, khaki cargo pants with dark contrast utility pockets and a fluorescent safety shirt, his short brown hair combed into respectable neatness. Tory smiled hello.

'Good morning to my two most special people,' Tory said as she walked to the kitchen bench, pulled a lunch box printed with fairies out from an under-bench cupboard, and opened a loaf of bread, taking out two slices.

'What do you want on your sandwiches today, Laura? Will cheese and Vegemite be alright again?'

'Yeah, that's okay, Mummy. Hey, in my lunch box, can you give me extra of those tiny muffins today? I want to trade with Bella. She loves them … pleeeease,' Laura pleaded, looking at Tory with wide eyes and an irresistibly cute smile.

'How can I say no to that face?' Tory laughed. 'And what will you be trading for one of my muffins?'

'She gets those fruit roll-ups, the ones you won't buy. I love them. You don't mind, do you?' Laura asked, scrunching her nose up, looking at her.

'I don't buy them because they are full of sugar. I suppose if you swap just once, it is okay,' Tory said, shaking her head. Out of the corner of her eye, she watched Laura's eyes light up as she did a tiny fist pump before going back to her breakfast.

While she packed Laura's lunch box, Brent walked behind her and wrapped his arms around her waist. Tory turned and stood on tiptoes to give him a quick kiss, leaving lipstick evidence.

'I'll take this out,' he said, wiping off the lipstick as he picked up yesterday's rubbish bag and headed towards the laundry.

A moment later, he walked back into the kitchen. 'Tors, did you forget to lock the back door?'

'Not that I can remember. I don't even think I went out there last night,' Tory replied, shrugging her shoulders.

'Who knows how long it's been unlocked? We've got to be more careful.'

Tory nodded and got ready to head off, urging Laura to grab her schoolbag and get in the car.

'Hey, did you move my handbag?' Tory called out to Brent from the bedroom. She suppressed a flare of annoyance. He was always moving things and not putting them back.

'Why would I do that?' Brent called back from the kitchen.

'Well, it's not where I put it,' Tory said. She looked under the bed, and the sense of unease returned. Worried, Tory walked to the front hallway, opened the door, and looked out. The garage door was open, and there was an empty space where her Honda should have been.

'Damn,' she swore.

Tory slammed the door shut and rushed back to the kitchen.

'It's gone. The car, it's gone,' she blurted to Brent.

With a sudden realisation, Tory understood why the back door was not locked and her handbag no longer sat on her bedside table. Her stomach clenched, and an icy shiver ran down her spine.

'Oh my God, they were inside the house. They were next to me in the bedroom while we slept,' Tory said. She gulped for air.

'Who was, Mummy?' Laura asked. Her face scrunched as if she was trying to figure out a puzzle.

Tory paled. 'I feel sick.'

Someone, a stranger, worse, a criminal stranger, entered her bedroom last night. They stood next to her while she slept. The intruders may have carried weapons; they could have done anything to them.

'Brent, what are we going to do? They might have hurt us, or worse, killed us!'

'I'll call the police.' Brent pulled his mobile phone out of his pocket.

Tory sat on a chair, bending forward, resting her head in her hands.

'Mummy.' Laura shook her arm. 'Mummy, are you okay? It will be alright,' Laura reassured her.

Tory looked at her wonderful daughter.

Oh God, they could have hurt her, she thought in panic.

Tory wrapped her arms around Laura and embraced her in a tight hug.

'Mummy, you're squishing me.' Laura twisted, trying to duck out of her mother's grip.

Tory, still breathing hard, released Laura.

Brent looked at them both, quickly assessing Tory's anxiety. He stepped forward, swept Laura up in his arms, and in a jovial voice told her, 'I'm going to treat you with a trip to school in the truck, young lady.'

As Brent walked out the door, he said over his shoulder, 'Tors, I'll be back in ten.'

Laura, with a big smile plastered on her face, waved to Tory as Brent carried her to his truck.

Tory knew people talked about feeling violated by having their space invaded. She never understood, until now, why they couldn't just be glad no one got hurt and get on with their lives. It was the 'what if?' The possibility something worse might have happened. The realisation of just how vulnerable you were. Asleep in your bed, not knowing an evil person was standing right over you. It was the stuff of nightmares. Images of the 'what ifs' plagued Tory's mind.

CHAPTER 2

A police wagon pulled up to the front of the house at the same time as Brent returned from dropping Laura at school. Tory noticed Brent didn't park in the garage. Perhaps he assumed the police would want him to keep away from the crime scene, she thought.

Tory watched from the lounge window as two uniformed police officers, a male and a female, met Brent in the driveway and shook his hand. Both officers looked very young. The male officer held a notebook and was writing notes as he listened to Brent. The female officer nodded as if she was agreeing with what he told them.

Tory opened the front door and walked out to meet them.

'As I said on the phone, the garage door was open when we went out this morning, and the car was gone,' she heard Brent say.

Brent offered the introductions. 'Tory, this is Sergeants James Long and Eliza Joyce.' The detectives nodded their greeting.

'Please call us James and Liz,' James said as he offered his hand to Tory to shake.

Tory invited the officers into the house. They walked into the kitchen's dining area. Brent pulled out a chair, indicating for them to sit around the table.

'Would anyone like a coffee or tea?' Tory asked.

Both officers shook their heads.

'No, thank you,' James said. 'We need to run through what happened. When you realised you were robbed, and anything that may be of interest leading up to that moment.'

The officers were compassionate and kind. Liz seemed concerned about Tory's welfare. She asked Tory several times if either of them was injured.

James took the lead in asking questions.

'Apart from Tory's handbag and car, was anything else stolen?'

'I've looked around the house and can't see anything missing. Brent still has his wallet and keys. Our phones were still on the charger in the kitchen. They didn't leave anything behind either, at least nothing we have noticed,' Tory said.

'Did you hear the roller door open?'

'No, of course not,' Brent said, his forehead creased into a frown. 'Otherwise, I would have checked it out at the time. The manual override to open the roller door was activated. They probably used Tory's keys to get into the garage in the first place. All my tools are still there. None of them were stolen. It's weird.'

'There was a party at the first house in the street, about four houses up, at number two. Music was playing well after we went to bed. Perhaps the party masked the intruder's noise?' Tory said.

'I doubt they did the break-in, though. They are good people,' Brent added.

'We will talk to them to see if they heard or saw anything,' Liz said.

'Were all the doors locked when you went to bed last night?' James asked.

'We think so. I don't recall checking the laundry door before going to bed, but we always lock it when we come back inside from there,' Brent said.

'I locked the front door and the sliding family-room door before we went to bed,' Tory said.

After they answered questions about the timing of events, James asked for specific details of what was taken.

'Tory, can you please make a detailed inventory of what was in your handbag, and anything in your car?'

'You'll probably fill a notebook listing what you had in your bag,' Brent said, looking at Tory as he gave a short laugh.

'Not funny,' Tory said. She scowled at him. 'Oh God, my purse. All my cards were in there. I can't even remember what they all were.'

'Take your time. There will be detectives assigned to this case once we report back to the station. Because you were in the house when the intruders robbed you, it's called an aggravated robbery. Senior police officers will take charge and investigate. You'll be in good hands,' James said.

'Aggravated robbery. That sounds so violent,' Tory said.

'It might have been if you had woken while the intruders were inside. This is something we see as a very serious crime and want to apprehend the intruders quickly.'

'I don't know if I should be grateful or horrified they didn't wake us.'

'As things have turned out, I would say grateful,' Liz said, her voice soft. 'There have been some pretty bad outcomes when the owners have been woken.'

Tory stared at Liz as she spoke, her mind leaping from one imagined scenario to another.

'You can give the list of handbag contents and anything else you realise has been stolen to the detectives when they come to talk to you, or email me at this address,' James said, handing Tory a business card and giving her a supportive smile. 'The forensic team will be here later today to dust for prints. The detectives will also come by today. Can you stay here for them?'

Tory and Brent nodded their assent.

Tory listened to the final questions, her mind in a fog. Brent answered on their behalf. Finished, the officers stood to leave.

'You'll need to call the bank and cancel your cards,' Liz reminded them as she followed her colleague out the door.

Tory watched from the doorway until the officers got into their police wagon and drove down the street before she closed the door.

'Caffeine will be required. I'll make coffee,' Brent said, giving her a hug. 'You make a list of things in your bag.'

'I can remember my credit cards, but I can't remember how many loyalty cards I had.'

'Does it matter?' Brent asked. 'What can they do with those anyway?'

'I don't know. I don't suppose my driver's licence is important either. They already know where I live.'

'Still, better report that one. Call the Services office soon. You don't want to get a fine for not having your licence with you when you drive,' Brent said. 'I am going to have another look around in case we missed something. Might chat to the neighbours and see if they heard anything, although the party up the road might make it tricky to decipher if anyone seen in the street were partygoers or thieves.'

Tory sat at the kitchen table and wrote her list as best she could. She sucked on the end of her pen as she tried to recall the contents of her purse. There were some cards she knew she'd forgotten but was out of ideas of what they might be. She put down the pen and picked up her phone from the bench to call the first bank. The protracted steps of the automated messages eventually connected her to a person to cancel her Visa card. An hour later, she leant back in relief, with three cards cancelled, a reissued driver's licence, and a Medicare card in the mail.

Tory looked up as Brent walked into the room.

'Everything takes so long,' she complained. 'In the time it takes to get put through to the right person to cancel the cards and then get them reissued, I feel like I could have walked to the bank and back. We still need to contact the insurance company. I'll do that next. How did you go? Did you find anything? Did they take anything else?'

'I had a good look. Nothing was out of place. I can't even see how they got in; there was no damage around the laundry door, so they didn't break the lock. They must have picked it, I guess, unless we really did leave it unlocked. I spoke to Reg next door and Lois on the other side, and they didn't hear or see anything. Reg said his dog was inside all night and didn't bark, although the dog is half deaf and nearly blind, so that's not much use to us.'

'It just seems so weird. I might understand it if my car was a luxury Lexus or Beamer, but it's just a little Honda Civic. They wouldn't have broken in just to steal the car. Surely not.'

'They got your cards. Perhaps they were the target, and the car was opportunistic. Who knows?' Brent said as he shrugged his shoulders.

* * *

Brent leant forward to put his arms around Tory's shoulders as she sat at the table. It tore at his heart to see her so distressed. Knowing someone was inside their home made Brent angry. The bastards would've copped a thumping if he woke last night. There was no way he would allow anyone to hurt Tory or Laura. It worried him that he didn't wake up when they were in the house. Despite Tory telling him he didn't wake up to Laura crying when she was a baby, he always considered himself a light sleeper. The thought of not waking up last night made him uneasy. He wondered if he would sleep through other emergencies. He resolved to test the smoke detectors that afternoon to ensure they worked.

'Hey, Tors, I think just to be on the safe side, we should charge our phones in the bedroom instead of the kitchen. That way, we have quick access to them if we need to call 000 while we're in bed.'

'Good idea,' Tory said, and rested her head along his arm.

'I'm going to have a look around the place to see if I can make it any more secure.' Brent kissed the top of Tory's head and squeezed her shoulder.

* * *

It surprised Tory when the two forensic police arrived an hour later. She didn't know what she was expecting but hadn't anticipated they would arrive so soon. They introduced themselves as Constables Grant McKimmie and Lucy Wright.

'It's terrible what has happened to you,' Constable Wright said to Tory. 'But unfortunately, it's not uncommon. We have more and more of these disturbances every month.'

Tory watched the pair step into white overalls with the word *'Forensic'* stencilled across the back. They made their way to the side of the house. The officers dusted for prints inside the laundry and on the outside of the door, leaving a fine, black layer of dust on everything they brushed.

'Looks like they were wearing gloves. We only found two sets of prints, which would be yours,' Constable McKimmie said, looking at them. 'The lock on the laundry door doesn't appear damaged. So, either you guys left it unlocked or they picked it. Those locks are pretty easy to unlock without a key, if you know how,' he said.

Brent and Tory eyed each other, the assumption making them uneasy.

'I don't reckon we left it unlocked,' Brent said. 'This arvo I'm going to get chains for the doors. Anything to make it harder for someone to break in, or at least wake us up if they are trying to.'

A knock at the front door interrupted them.

'I'll get it,' Tory said as she walked to the door.

Standing on the front porch were two detectives.

The female spoke in a deep voice.

'Hello. I am Detective Robyn Blunt,' she said as she held out her hand for Tory to shake. She turned to the man next to her and introduced him as her partner, Detective Peter Morgan.

The woman was taller than her partner and more athletic-looking. Her mid-length brown hair was tied back in a no-nonsense pigtail. Tory guessed she was in her mid-thirties. She walked with an air of command, clearly the leader of the two. Detective Morgan was older, perhaps in his mid-forties, with a medium build and strong, square shoulders. Sunglasses were pushed back on top of his curly auburn hair. Both wore dark blue suits and sturdy boots. Detective Blunt wore a white shirt under her tailored jacket, while Detective Morgan wore a striped shirt and tie. Detective Morgan's eyes were intense, and as he looked at her, Tory shivered under his scrutiny.

Brent and Tory sat with the detectives at their dining table, where they repeated much of what they had told the other police officers earlier that morning. The detectives asked them to go into greater detail.

'Do you know if any of your neighbours have security cameras?'

'Not to my knowledge. I don't think so,' Brent said. 'I haven't seen any or any signs warning there are cameras at a house, but I don't know for sure.'

'What about you, Tory?' Detective Blunt said.

'Same as Brent. I don't think so, but I haven't had any reason to ask them about cameras before today.'

The detectives continued to ask questions for an hour before the forensic officers interrupted their meeting, motioning the detectives aside for a brief exchange. The detectives nodded at what they were told before waving as the forensic team let themselves out of the house.

'No fingerprints on the laundry door, other than yours, means they were wearing gloves, which is not surprising, even if they were amateurs. However, considering their lock-picking skills, if indeed the door was locked, it's likely they are experienced thieves,' Detective Blunt said.

A few questions later, the interview concluded.

'We will need to meet with you both again as the investigation progresses,' Detective Morgan said.

'In the meantime, if you remember anything you would like to add to the information you told us today, please call or email me,' Detective Blunt said as she handed Tory a business card.

'They seemed nice,' Tory said after the detectives left.

'Yeah, they did. They seemed to care about what happened and were keen to find the intruders,' Brent said.

Tory made a coffee and carried her cup outside to the patio while Brent went to the local hardware store. She sat on a wicker chair and looked over the small, neat yard. Tory felt stressed, and the peace of the yard held a somewhat calming effect. Although it was late summer, the flower garden was still in bloom and looked pretty. The house they rented was one they would love to buy if they could save enough for a deposit. It was a renovated three-bedroom home built in the late seventies. It was comfortable and on a nice street. The main bedroom sat at the front of the house, and on the other side of the kitchen and family room was Laura's room, with the spare bedroom at the back.

At the side of the house, the external door of the laundry opened to the clothesline and an area where three rubbish bins were kept. Further on was a gate that led to the front garden.

It puzzled Tory that she hadn't heard the side gate being opened.

With a deep, drawn-out sigh, Tory stood and walked back into the house. She pulled the insurance papers from a kitchen drawer and made the call.

* * *

'We don't pay out the insurance on car theft for thirty days, unless the car is located earlier.'

'That long? I will need a car before then.' Tory paced the room while listening.

'There was an option on your policy for a hire car, but you didn't choose it, so I am afraid I can't offer you one.'

Shit. Shit, thought Tory.

'If your car is located and it's damaged, we will arrange an assessor to look at it. After that, we can complete a payment or repairs to the vehicle. The value we have on your vehicle is $8,600.'

'Oh, is that all? It cost a lot more three years ago.'

'Yes, $8,600 is the book value we have. If there is anything else I can do for you, please don't hesitate to call back.'

'Thanks for nothing,' Tory muttered as she disconnected the call.

What was she going to do without a car for thirty days? Tory sat on a dining chair and massaged her temples, trying to stave off a developing headache.

CHAPTER 3

'I bought two sets of chains, one for each of the external doors. Luckily, I got a trade discount,' Brent told Tory as he strode into the house, holding the chains out to show her.

With Brent's arrival, Tory felt herself relax. Brent dropped the chains on the kitchen bench and held his arms out to embrace Tory.

'You've had a tough morning, babe.'

'The worst.'

'It will be alright, Tors. You'll see.'

'A-ha,' she mumbled. 'Can I help you attach the chains?'

'Nah, you can sit back and watch the master at work,' Brent said. He puffed out his chest and bobbed his head from side to side, his blue eyes twinkling as he turned from her, picked up the chains, and headed to the laundry.

'Brent, do you think the landlord will mind us putting on the chains?'

'Nah, I don't reckon they will mind. It enhances the place. If they do, I can always remove the chains when we move out.'

Tory liked to watch Brent work. He had what his mother called 'pianist's hands'. Long, elegant fingers that would have been perfect for playing the piano, if he'd had an inkling to do so. Slim and fit, he was taller than her by ten centimetres. Tory found herself attracted to his powerful shoulders, that and his cheeky grin. Laura inherited her pale complexion from her father, although now, after working outdoors all summer, Brent's skin was tanned. He was a skilled carpenter whose work was in demand. He'd been at the same company since completing his apprenticeship and had an easy and friendly relationship with his workmates.

Chains installed, Brent turned to her.

'All done. They might be tricky to get on and off because I shortened the chains a bit to make it harder to open the door very far. I don't want someone able to push bolt cutters through the door crack and cut the chain. Try it. See if you can get them to work.'

Tory stepped forward, unhooked the chain from its catch and then re-hooked it.

'Good. They'll work okay. Laura might struggle, but I am happy not to let her out too easy,' Brent said with a smile.

'Do you think we should buy security cameras?' Tory was still worried.

'Possibly, but they are expensive. We will need to up our internet plan too if we get them.'

'I guess cameras wouldn't have stopped someone coming into the bedroom, though, would they? Let's stick with the chains for now. Maybe we can get the cameras later?'

'They are not likely to come back again anyway. I reckon they got what they wanted last night,' Brent said.

CHAPTER 4

Brent dropped Tory at her work and drove off with a wave. Tory smiled to herself as she recalled that morning's intimacy with her hot husband. She walked through the familiar showroom of Jensen's Heating & Cooling to the shared office space towards the back of the building. The showroom comprised half a dozen samples of heaters and air conditioners, several with external covers removed to show the inner workings of the unit. Large, bright posters and display banners lined the walls, and a reception desk sat along the back wall next to the doorway leading to the office space. Tory nodded a hello to the friendly receptionist, who was busy chatting on the phone as she passed.

Tory loved her work. It made her feel successful and important. It also served as a sanctuary of sorts when Laura was hounding her. Working with the team of sixteen people was fun, and she sensed Frank, the boss, held a soft spot for her. Frank accepted her application when she wanted to leave her old job and get out of the rat race in Sydney, and Tory was grateful for the chance he took on employing her based on an interview over a video conference. Today, he looked much the same as he did when she first met him. Short brown hair, greying at the temples, wearing long black pants, tan work boots, and a yellow polo shirt with the company logo embroidered on the right-hand side. The polo stretched tight over his generous belly. When she called yesterday, telling him she wouldn't be able to come to work because of the robbery, he expressed understanding and concern.

Frank had promoted her to credit manager last month, which meant an extra hundred dollars in the payslip each fortnight. Brent was thrilled when she proudly told him the good news.

Looking around the office, Tory thought it could do with a brightening up. A photo of Brent and Laura was next to her computer, and a large pot plant, with wilting leaves, sat on the floor. The walls were a dull grey, and the fluorescent lighting removed any warmth from the atmosphere.

Tory was still shaken by the robbery. Last night she lay in bed, unable to sleep. Every sound made her sit up and listen harder, trying to detect if someone was in the house. She got out of bed three or four times to check Laura was safe and to double-check the chains were still on the locked doors. When morning arrived, Tory was exhausted. She could see panda eyes staring back at her in the mirror as she cleaned her teeth. Tory hoped work would keep her mind off yesterday's events.

A commotion in the showroom caused Tory to turn toward the doorway. Carolyn, her best friend, walked in fifteen minutes late, carrying a large, exquisite bunch of flowers. Not acknowledging her lateness, and with a huge grin on her face, she walked past Frank and almost pounced on the bookkeeper, Rita, who turned sixty-one today.

'Happy birthday, beautiful lady,' she exhaled as she handed the flowers to Rita. Carolyn reached into her tote bag and pulled out a small, pretty jar with a pink bow around the top. She offered it to Rita.

'Here is an essential oil I made from my roses last weekend, so you can smell as beautiful as you look, my lovely. It will last a few years, if you don't use it all at once.'

Tory saw Frank smile. He could see how special this made Rita feel, and Tory knew he recognised the joy Carolyn brought to the office. He would overlook her being late this time, and probably the next.

'So,' said one of the guys in the office, 'tell us what else you got up to on the weekend, Caro.' Carolyn always had grand stories of party nights out, or some story of a desperately sad man standing her up. She was a beautiful woman, tall and slim, with long blonde hair, a lovely, kind personality, and a great sense of fun. She always looked stunning in everything she wore. Today she wore green print trousers with a matching sleeveless body-hugging top, her hair piled high in a loose bun on top of her head, all of which accentuated her slimness and height. Carolyn attracted men, and the guys in the office were keen to hear about her life, particularly her partying lifestyle.

Tory laughed to herself. What Carolyn did wasn't half as exciting as she made it sound. Still, Tory wouldn't get in the way of a good story.

Most people who knew her well called her Caro. She was a loyal friend to Tory. Both celebrated their twenty-eighth birthdays late last year. They met not long after Tory moved to the area seven years ago, when she saw Carolyn at the local markets, working at a stall selling perfumes and essential oils. Tory approached her stall, and Carolyn told her she made the goods she was selling. After the markets, they caught up for coffee, and Tory discovered Carolyn was having a hard time after her boyfriend dumped her, leaving her pregnant, alone, and feeling worthless. Tory supported her through the abortion and recommended Carolyn to Frank when a vacancy arose at work. Carolyn was eternally grateful to Tory.

'Hi, girlfriend. What happened to you yesterday?' Carolyn said. She sat on the edge of Tory's desk.

'Oh, Caro, you won't believe it. We were robbed.'

'Seriously! What did they take? Are you all okay?'

'We are fine. They stole my car and handbag. I was going to call you, but ended up so exhausted with all the running around, I didn't.' Tory wanted to stop thinking about the robbery and just get on with work, but she knew she needed to tell Carolyn the full story, so she started from the beginning.

'Wow, that's intense. I am glad you guys are not hurt. Is Laura okay?'

Laura idolised Carolyn, and the love was returned in buckets. Carolyn would take any opportunity to care for Laura or to treat her in some way. Laura loved staying over at Carolyn's small home.

Tory remembered the first time she visited Carolyn's home years ago, not long after they met, and Caro was still living with her nan. It was only in the past six months that Nan had moved into the nursing home. Tory remembered walking into the backyard of the small home and gasping.

'It is magnificent,' she said to Carolyn, looking from one side of the yard to the other. Bright blooms filled the beautiful garden. Tory inhaled the sweet scent of the flowers. Garden beds edged with gorgeous stone paths wove their way to a small rotunda standing under the canopy of two trees. It was a perfect spot for a person to sit and take in the perfume and colour. The dappled shade provided by the trees created a cool space to enjoy the beauty while sipping a coffee or wine. She imagined living here would be like living in a perfumed wonderland. Laura called it a 'fairy paradise' and loved to play in it every opportunity she got.

Nan used her husband's life insurance to buy this small cottage after his death a few decades ago. As part of her grieving process, Nan threw herself into gardening and created the most beautiful garden Tory had ever seen. Carolyn inherited Nan's green thumb, and the garden still looked just as perfect now, despite Nan no longer living there.

Nan and Carolyn shared a special bond. Carolyn's parents moved to New Zealand for work when she was thirteen. They never returned, and Carolyn grew into adulthood living with Nan. Nan was chuffed that Carolyn shared her love of gardening and promised to leave the house and garden to her when she passed. Carolyn missed her old housemate. They talked regularly on the phone, and Carolyn visited the nursing home every week.

'Do the police think they will find the intruders?' Carolyn asked.

'They didn't really talk much about that. They told me so many things, I have forgotten half of them. I'm still in shock at someone being in my bedroom while we slept.'

Carolyn moved next to Tory and gave her a reassuring hug.

'You'll be okay now. Don't let it worry you.'

Tory could see the concern in her friend's face and tried to smile. She didn't want Carolyn to be concerned for her.

A short, tapping sound interrupted their conversation. They looked up through the clear glass partition into Frank's office. He looked their way with an impatient frown on his face.

'Time to get to work, sister,' Carolyn said as she gracefully moved to her desk. 'Talk more at lunch.'

CHAPTER 5

One day without Tory's car, and they seemed to hit one obstacle after another. After work, in the evening, Tory and Brent sat at the dining table.

'It's as if we need a contingency plan for life,' Tory moaned.

'You and I need to get to work and Laura to school, all at different times. One car isn't going to cut it. I'll go late to work for a bit and take Laura to school, and you can get a lift with your workmates. I can pick Laura up except for footy training nights.'

'What if you missed one training night?'

Pre-season training with the football club was in full swing, and Brent was a committed footballer.

'I could, but a spot in the team is hard to secure, and it might be weeks before you get a car. I can't miss many sessions, or I won't have a hope of getting selected.'

'So, what can we do?'

'I'll call Mum and see if she's able to pick up Laura. She can bring her here until you get home.'

Tory grimaced. Gail would love that. Her mother-in-law took

every opportunity to criticise her, and she knew Gail would see this as her failure to parent.

'If you have to. I suppose there is no other choice,' Tory said.

'It will be alright, Tors. Laura will love it.'

Yes, but will I? Tory thought.

Tory felt Brent's mother was always pointedly suggesting her own marriage was one Brent and Tory should aspire to.

Thirty-five years ago, short, dumpy Gail married tall, somewhat dorky Gordon in the one church in their hometown in rural NSW. Their little town, Bowagong, comprised a corner store, the church, a pub, and a football team. Brent grew up there. He attended the local primary school, and when he and his mates progressed to high school, they travelled by bus to the nearest school in Aloma.

In Brent's childhood home, despite her being older, greyer, still dumpy, and now unfit, Gail ruled the household. Tory always sensed Gail held expectations she couldn't live up to, from the number of grandchildren she should provide to how she should care for Brent and Laura. Around Gail, Tory always felt 'observed' and inadequate. Tory tried to bite her tongue and get along, but some days it took all the willpower she had to stay silent.

'Always happy to help when needed,' Gail told Brent.

* * *

Fuming, Tory met Brent at the door as he returned home from training.

'She did it again, only this time it was the entire house. She vacuumed, dusted, and ironed the clothes in the basket. The house

I run doesn't meet her standards. I am not good enough to be your wife. And then she says to Laura, *"Mummy is sooo busy; she obviously can't keep up with the housework."* What about you? Nothing said about your vacuuming skills or ability to iron!'

Brent smiled at her. 'She's just trying to help. Don't take it the wrong way. Dad didn't do any housework when I lived there.'

'Yes, but she didn't have a job!'

While grateful Gail could help with Laura, she found her feelings of inadequacy around Gail exhausting.

Tory crossed her arms. 'The sooner I get my car situation sorted out, the better.'

* * *

Brent's jaw clenched as he watched Tory storm off. Tory and his mother clashed from the moment he and Tory were married. He couldn't understand why she let Gail upset her so much. He wondered if they were too much alike, both infuriatingly independent and strong-willed. Brent knew his mum sometimes was bossy, but she always did nice things for them. Gail adored Laura, and he was grateful when she could help out. As far as he was concerned, coming home to a cooked meal or a clean house was a bonus. It saved him from doing his share of it. He didn't understand why Tory pushed back. They both worked hard and didn't always have time to cook nice meals. He'd never heard his mother say anything unkind to Tory.

'She's undermining me, Brent. She's trying to show me up, make me look inadequate,' Tory said.

Brent didn't agree. He wondered if it was some sort of lack of confidence on Tory's part, or perhaps it had something to do with Tory not having her own mother to turn to?

'She loves us all. You too, Tors. Mum just wants to help.'

'She needs to ask what we want for help, not just do things. She's always implying I don't do things properly, and I don't look after you or Laura in the way it should be done. It makes me feel like shit.'

'Tors, babe, don't be like that. I'll talk to her, try to get her to just look after Laura, not take over the household. Okay?'

Tory's nod didn't convince Brent he'd calmed her. Her arms remained crossed, and she still frowned. He wondered if they could resolve things if the two of them just sat down and talked about it.

Yeah, right. All he needed to do was work up enough courage, and probably kiss sex goodbye for a month, to make that suggestion to Tory.

CHAPTER 6

Tory arrived home puffing after the short walk from the end of their street, where her colleague dropped her after work. She stepped into the kitchen doorway and saw Brent and Laura playing 'cooks' with a pan boiling on the stovetop and Laura, an apron wrapped around her tiny waist, following Brent around the kitchen. Utensils and remnants of ingredients pulverised on the chopping board covered the bench. She loved this, coming home to domestic bliss. Watching Brent and Laura interacting in an adult-like way made her realise just how fast her daughter was growing up. Her heart burst with love for them both.

'Hi, beautiful people. Mmm, something smells good.'

'Hi, Mummy. We are making spaghetti *bognase*. I am in charge of the cheese,' Laura said as she held up the parmesan for her to see.

Brent leant in to give Tory a kiss.

'Hi, Tors. Good day?'

'The usual. Nothing too exciting. Although Caro and Karl seem to be flirting a bit seriously. I think something might be cooking there.'

Karl was an electrician at Tory's work and a full forward in Brent's football team.

'Hah! Good on Karl. They would be a nice couple, I reckon. Hey, there's mail on the table for you,' Brent said. He gestured toward the table.

Tory swept the two letters up, offering both a quick glance.

'Looks like junk mail, but oddly they're addressed to you,' Brent added.

'Oh, look at this,' Tory said, waving the letter from the first opened envelope. 'Apparently, I have opened a credit card account; they are thanking me for being a customer. Sweet.'

'Tors,' Brent said, his voice cautious. 'That may not be junk. It might be real, you know, from having your info stolen.'

Tory paused, and her eyes met Brent's. 'Oh crap, I didn't think of that. I'd better call them and see what they say.'

Tory picked her mobile phone off the bench, walked into the lounge room where it was quiet, and dialled the number on the letter.

Ten minutes later, Brent looked up from the stove as Tory walked back into the kitchen.

'Tors, what is it? You look shattered.'

'The company said they received an online application with all my details. They approved the card with a limit of ten thousand dollars! That's more credit than I would ever apply for.'

'Did they cancel the card?'

'Yes, and told me I should go to the police. They also said I was lucky the thieves hadn't changed my address on the driver's licence they used as identification. Otherwise, the company would have sent the card and letter to the new address, and I wouldn't have known a thing about it. How can companies give away credit cards without checking with the person first?'

'I suppose they had enough details the company thought it was legit?'

'I don't know. It seems too easy. When I wanted a card, I had to prove my income and just about offer my firstborn as collateral. These people just got the card like that,' Tory said, snapping her fingers.

'You've cancelled your driver's licence, right?' Brent asked.

'I got a replacement one issued, but they don't normally change the actual licence number. Shit. I'll call them now and see if I can get one with a new number.'

Worried, Brent said, 'I am afraid to ask, Tors. What was the other letter?'

'It was junk mail, thank goodness. Someone trying to sell me tyres. If I had a car, they could've had a chance! We've got to do something about getting me a car soon. I don't know how long I can keep juggling things,' Tory added. 'Bloody insurance. Thirty days is hopeless.'

'Okay, we can talk about the car later. First things first. It's probably too late after hours to get onto the licence people, but you'd better call the police now.'

Tory made the call. Detective Blunt was finished for the day, so she spoke to another police officer who took the details and promised to leave a message for the detective. Tory's stolen wallet had now escalated to identity theft.

After Tory finished her call with the police, she sat on the couch, her head resting in her trembling hands. Someone had her identity. What would they do with it next?

Laura ran into the lounge room.

'Dinner's ready, Mummy.'

Tory lifted her head and smiled at her daughter. 'Thank you, darling.'

She took her hand, and they walked to the dining table.

'Tors, let's eat first, then you should call the banks to let them know, just in case they get credit applications over the weekend,' Brent said.

Tory was quiet as they ate. She let Laura's nonstop chatter wash over her. After dinner, she took Laura to her bed and kissed her.

'Goodnight, darling. Sleep tight.'

'Night, Mummy.'

Back in the dining room, Tory pulled out her mobile phone and called her two banks on their twenty-four-hour number. The staff on both calls were reassuring, telling Tory she was right to call immediately when she found out about the fraudulent credit card.

The second helpline person, Nathan, was particularly friendly and made Tory feel confident with what she was being told.

'Thank you for your support,' Tory said. 'While you're on the phone, can you tell me when the two replacement cards for the ones I had stolen will arrive? It's been pretty inconvenient without a savings or credit card.'

'Tory, the cards were sent five days ago. You should've received them by now,' replied her new friend Nathan.

'They haven't arrived.'

'Can you confirm your address, please?' Nathan asked.

Tory relayed it to him.

'I am sorry, Tory. The address on file is a different one. It appears your address was updated recently. Did you do that?'

'No. Oh shit. Does this mean my cards have been mailed to another address? Where did you send them?'

'Unfortunately, Tory, I can't tell you over the phone.'

'Can you change my address back, please?' Tory was anxious now. Brent heard the tension in her voice and put his arms around her.

'I can't do that. You will need to come into the bank on Monday with evidence of your current address for me to change it. Your driver's licence and a utility bill of some sort with your address on it will be fine.'

Tory wanted to shout at him. Her bloody driver's licence needed to be cancelled.

'Can you at least cancel the new cards, so they don't get used?'

'Yes, I am doing that now as we speak. Again, I am sorry, Tory. This must be very upsetting for you,' Nathan said.

'How did they change my address? Can you tell where this was done? Was it in person?'

'I am not sure. To change it back now, you need to attend your local branch as soon as you can. You have to do this in person. Is there anything else I can do for you, Tory?'

'No. Thanks for your help,' Tory said, gritting her teeth as she ended the call. She was pissed. So pissed off she thought her head might explode.

'Damn it, Brent. I have to go to the bank on Monday now. Those creeps have changed my address with the bank. They probably have my new cards, which are now cancelled, again. I will have to wait another week or so to get new cards.'

It was unbelievable. A complete stranger could change her address on her, but she couldn't change it back!

Brent pulled her towards him in a hug. 'Tors, it will be okay. When you are at the bank, ask them to hang onto the cards till you come in to pick them up. That way you can be sure they get to you.'

She put her head on his shoulder. 'When will this end? It's completely nuts, and bloody inconvenient. Without a card, I am going to need you to get me some cash out so I can pay for things.'

'Can do. I'll go to the ATM in the morning. Let's go to bed now and worry about things tomorrow.'

Tory nodded distractedly as she headed to the bedroom; she had a sinking feeling tomorrow would be worse.

CHAPTER 7

Tory spent another night unable to sleep. She tossed in bed, her mind conjuring scenarios of dread. She felt sick thinking about the security of their savings, all the money they were saving to buy their new house. If the fraudsters could get credit cards in her name and change her address at the bank, would they be able to access their savings? It was in a fixed deposit, with a requirement that both she and Brent needed to sign for any withdrawal. Was it possible for the fraudsters to change that condition? She didn't know anymore. Not so long ago, she assumed their money was secure. One thing was for sure: from now on, they were going to need to monitor their bank accounts more closely.

Tory rose early before the others woke, made a coffee, and sat at their computer. She searched the internet for ways to improve their financial security. Tory looked up as Brent walked in a while later, showered and dressed for work.

'Morning.'

'Morning, babe. What are you doing up so early?'

'I couldn't sleep, so I decided to do some banking research. Did you know through the banking app, we can set up an alert system on our phones for when there is a transaction from one of the accounts?' Tory said.

'Really? That seems sensible. We can do that. Why haven't we already done it?'

'If I knew it was possible, I would have,' Tory said. 'Hand me your phone. I'll set both ours up now.'

Tory updated the settings on both their phones.

'Done,' Tory said. She handed Brent his phone. 'If any withdrawals show up on the joint account you're not sure about, call me first, I guess. We don't want to cancel a valid transaction by mistake.'

'Will do. Thanks, Tors.' Brent bent and kissed her on the forehead.

Tory felt marginally better. With the messaging in place, they could monitor for anything unexpected, and then if they saw something odd, get in contact with the bank immediately.

* * *

It was early Sunday afternoon when Carolyn knocked at the door for a welcome visit. Smiling, Tory opened the door. She was glad to see her friend.

'Hi, Caro,' Tory said as she gave her a hug.

'Hi, girlfriend. I believe you need a distraction. I'm going to fill you in on my man crush and play with Laura, all with a glass of wine in hand,' she said, her smile wide as she pulled a bottle of chardonnay out of her oversized handbag.

'Wine o'clock it is!' Tory smiled, grateful for the lighthearted distraction.

Tory took the wine in one hand and, with her other hand, grabbed two glasses from the kitchen cupboard before walking outside to the patio table. She called out to Laura, 'Darling, Caro is here. She has something to show you.'

Laura ran out to the patio and flung her arms around Carolyn.

'Hey, beautiful girl, how are you?' Carolyn returned the hug.

'Hello. I'm good. What have you got to show me?' Laura squealed with excitement.

'Today we are going to make perfume.'

'Oooh, that will be dope. I can make some for my teacher. It's Mrs Cartwright's birthday soon.'

'Dope, huh?' Carolyn said. She suppressed a smile, raising her eyebrows at Tory. Tory grinned back.

'Okay, Laura lovey, find the prettiest-smelling flowers you can, pick six or so, and bring them over here,' Carolyn instructed.

They sat, and Tory poured the wine. Glass in hand, Tory watched as Laura, with a look of concentration on her face, spent the next fifteen minutes walking from one flower to the next, smelling the centre of each.

'How are you faring?' Carolyn asked.

'Sometimes I wonder if I might be going crazy. I am so worried about the security of our finances, and the bloody car insurance delay is driving me mad. Everything is a constant juggle. It's a nightmare that I can't wake from. Brent's mother is helping, but that just makes things worse. She is always out to diminish me in one way or another. A few days ago, she told Laura to gather all her dirty clothes so she could take them home to wash, as I didn't have time to do it. She makes me sound useless. I get so angry with her.' Tory forced a smile toward Laura, who waved happily at them from the back of the yard.

'Well, just yell out if there is anything I can do to help.'

'You are doing it already,' Tory said and raised the glass in her hand with a smile.

Laura returned to them, her eyebrows furrowed in concentration.

'I like this one. It smells the best. Is that right?' Laura said, pointing to a rose and looking to Carolyn for approval. She smiled when Carolyn nodded to her.

'Good choice, Laura.'

Laura picked six flowers and placed them with care into the cheesecloth bag Carolyn held out to her.

'Now, you need to put the bag of petals in a bowl of water overnight. Tomorrow after school, Mummy can help you take the bag out. Give it a squeeze so the water stays in the bowl, and then boil the water until there is only a small amount left. When it cools, you can pour it into this pretty bottle and dab the perfume on yourself every morning.'

'Thanks, Caro. The bottle is soooo pretty. I am going to put it on my dressing table now, so it can wait for the perfume.' Laura skipped off to her room.

Tory laughed. 'Thanks for that, Caro. She will pretend she's a princess putting on perfume every morning.'

'My pleasure. Just remember the perfume will only last a few months tops, so make sure she uses it up pretty quickly.'

'Hang on.' Tory looked at Carolyn, puzzled. 'A few months? You told Rita her perfume would last a few years?'

'Different stuff,' Carolyn said, sipping her wine. 'Laura's is rose water. Rita's was essential oils. I made Rita's with the still. I boil the flowers in the still, add some magic spirits, extract the oils, and voila! It's much trickier to make, but it's a true concentrate of perfume. It keeps longer.'

'Of course, I should have realised that. I still struggle to picture you using the still. How is Nan going?' Tory asked.

'Nan's good. She likes it there. She keeps the nurses on their toes and is best friends with the gardener.'

* * *

Carolyn missed Nan. It was a hard decision to move her into the aged care facility. But it was a move of necessity, triggered after a cascading number of accidents. The last incident left Nan injured and unable to use her bandaged hand, necessitating assistance with pretty much all of life's functions. Carolyn wasn't able to be around her enough. Although she arranged for a caregiver to visit their home daily, she felt guilty every time she left for work. While Nan was physically deteriorating, her mind was sharp. It was Nan who recognised the burden she placed on her granddaughter and suggested to Carolyn that it was time she went into aged care. It was a confronting conversation for them both. However, over a few weeks, they came to the mutual understanding that it was the right decision. They were fortunate to find a lovely home with a garden where Nan could spend hours sitting and viewing the flowers and insect life. Carolyn knew the garden was a significant reason Nan was happy in her new home.

It was Nan who taught and inspired Carolyn's love of gardening. Together they spent many hours weeding, pruning, and propagating. Carolyn recalled with affection that it was Nan's idea to make perfume. There was a time when Carolyn didn't have a job. She was frustrated, looking for work and becoming despondent.

'Why don't you use all these plants to make money?' Nan asked her one day. 'Try making perfume and soaps using the fragrant plants.'

With no idea of where to start, the pair spent hours searching the internet for instructions. They discovered they needed a still. Carolyn ordered one online, with Nan providing the funds.

It was exciting when the parcel arrived.

'It looks like there might be some fumes from the still, and if something goes wrong, it does look a little dangerous,' Nan said, eyeing the glassware and tubes. 'How about we set it up in the garage?'

And so they did. Carolyn and Nan carried a little workbench they had been using for potting plants into the garage. There was enough room at the back of the garage behind Nan's car to set up the still.

'I'll back the car out when you want to use it, just in case something goes wrong,' Nan said, her eyes twinkling. Carolyn saw she was itching to see the thing work.

Nan brought in two outdoor folding chairs and sat with Tory, who had arrived to share in the excitement. Together they watched Carolyn as she built the still, with its glass tubes and beakers sitting over a small gas burner. Tory laughed at Carolyn, telling her, 'All you need is a white lab coat and safety glasses, and you'd be called Julius Sumner Miller.'

Distilling oils was not as easy as she first thought. Three weeks later, Carolyn needed to order another conical flask, having burned dry the still on her second attempt. It took many attempts to perfect her technique. It also took a long time to collect enough oils to sell. Carolyn did plan to buy a bigger copper still at some point, but they were expensive, so she hadn't ordered one yet.

Carolyn couldn't wipe the smile off her face as she watched Nan blush with pleasure when she gifted her the first sample of quality oil, prettied up in a decorative glass vial with a ribbon tied around it.

'Bless you, darling,' she said to Carolyn, giving her a hug. Carolyn was proud of herself, too. This batch of oil smelled perfect. She used the right plant, dried it properly, and she hadn't burned it.

* * *

Tory was as delighted for Laura, learning how to make the perfumed water. She loved that Caro took time to teach Laura about the garden when she stayed with her, and now, how to make the perfume. Tory wished she'd had someone to guide and teach her when she was a child. One day, when Laura was older, Caro might show her how to extract the oils in the still, Tory thought.

Tory had never actually seen Carolyn working the still because, as she explained to her, 'It takes hours to extract a tiny amount of essential oil from the plant. I need to monitor everything to make sure nothing goes wrong with the heat and the boiling process. Like blowing up the house.' Carolyn grinned at her. 'I can't have you or anyone distracting me.'

Tory looked at her best friend.

'You are a very special and talented lady, oh wise Caro. Now, tell me about your man crush.'

The afternoon passed quickly. Tory felt herself relax as the wine took effect.

'Alright, I'd better be off. If I have another wine, I won't be able to drive.'

'Thanks for coming, Caro. You are a star.'

Tory stood waving to Carolyn as she backed the car out of the drive. The phone in her pocket dinged. Tory glanced at her phone message as she turned to walk inside.

$600 payment made ….

Tory paled as she ran to find Brent.

CHAPTER 8

Tory arrived at work an hour early on Monday. She wanted to accrue time before going to the bank. Frank reluctantly supported Tory taking more time away from the office, provided she made up the hours. The bank was close to work, and Tory stood at the door right on opening time.

Later, at home, as she described to Brent what happened, Tory's blood pressure increased for the second time that day.

'At first, I got some guy who knew nothing about our situation, even though he was able to bring up our details on the computer. I explained again how our cards had been stolen and then how the thieves used my identity to create fraudulent applications and change my address. It then took me another thirty minutes to convince him to update the address with our current one. I'd taken the cancelled driver's licence and, luckily, our electricity and phone bills for him to see our address. Eventually, he changed it back. I asked him if it was possible to put some sort of alert on my account so it couldn't be changed again without me doing it in person and only at the local branch. He wasn't sure and told me he would investigate and get back to me. At least I was able to arrange the next lot of credit cards to be picked up in person from the bank.'

'Frustrating day, then,' Brent said. 'Come here, and I will give you a back rub, help you relax.'

'That would be nice. Thank you, babe. You are so very good to me.'

As Brent massaged her, Tory thought back to simpler times, when they'd first met. Carolyn had talked her into doing a charity fun run, and they trained for weeks. The ten-kilometre run was definitely not fun, in Tory's opinion. The only good thing about the day was meeting Brent. He ran the race without stopping, of course. Fit from training for football, he and his mates crushed the run. Meanwhile, Carolyn and Tory walked the last five kilometres. Both looked ridiculous in the fairy costumes they wore to celebrate the charity. At the finish line, Tory looked up to see Brent grinning at her. He walked over and started talking to them, not taking his eyes off her. Carolyn quickly took the hint and walked away to 'get a drink', not to return for half an hour. Brent asked her out on a date, and they never looked back.

Brent was sympathetic when Tory told him she never knew her father and her mother passed away when she was seventeen.

'My brother disappeared around then, too. I have no idea where he is. I moved to Sydney, got a job serving in a restaurant, and found a space in a share house. I enrolled in TAFE and did a certificate in business administration. Later, I got a job at a local car dealer for a while, didn't love it, and decided to get out of the city rat race. I applied for jobs randomly, all in regional areas, and got the one at Jensen's Heating & Cooling, so here I am.'

* * *

Brent felt sorry for Tory not having a family. His family bond was strong, and he found it hard to imagine life without that connection. He was determined to provide Tory with the family she didn't have in her youth. To provide the love and protection family afforded.

They were dating for a year when Tory accidentally fell pregnant with Laura. He couldn't have been more excited and proposed at once. His mother's reaction surprised and disappointed him.

'Brent, it's too soon. You hardly know her.'

'Mum, I love her, and she's pregnant. I want to do the right thing.'

'Doing the right thing doesn't necessarily mean you have to marry her, Brent.'

Brent was momentarily taken aback. It hadn't been what he expected her to say.

'Don't say anything else, please, Mum. I am going to marry her. I want to.'

He figured his parents would get used to the idea eventually. They had no choice.

They got married and continued to build a strong relationship. Last night, they'd talked about having another child. Both wanted a sibling for Laura.

'I think we need to be careful for a while, until this ID fraud is sorted,' Tory had recently said.

Brent agreed. 'We need financial security if you're going to stop working to care for another baby. Hopefully, things will get sorted soon.'

'I can't wait to try again,' Tory said as she nuzzled into the crook of his neck.

* * *

The issues at the bank earlier that day highlighted to Tory their financial vulnerability. The criminals weren't just trying to use her cancelled credit cards; they were creating more in her name. She needed her situation resolved so she could move on with her life. Tory felt a bit annoyed she hadn't heard from the police since leaving her message last Friday. As she walked from the kitchen, Tory noticed the business card Detective Blunt had handed her sitting on the desk.

Idiot. I should've called this mobile number instead of the general station number.

After she put Laura in bed, Tory picked up the detective's card and called the number.

'Detective Blunt speaking.'

'Hi, Detective. I am sorry to call you after hours, but my life has been crazy today, and I've been too busy to call before now,' Tory said. 'Is it okay to talk to you now?'

'Yes, I've finished for the day, but I'm happy to talk now. Has something happened, Tory?'

'I left a message for you last week. Didn't you get it?'

'I am sorry, I didn't. I'm not sure why. I'll look into it. Tell me what happened?'

'Whoever took my purse and cards has now used them to pretend to be me. They changed my address with the bank, and my new credit cards were sent to the new address. On top of that, I got a letter thanking me for applying for a new credit card, which I didn't do. I've spent the past few days trying to sort it out.'

'Okay, Tory, stay calm. I understand this can be very traumatic.

Did you cancel the card you didn't apply for and fix things with the bank?'

'Yes, but I don't have much confidence in the bank. I'm worried they will let someone change the address again.'

'I'm sorry I can't help you with the bank and their procedures. I can assure you, though, that the police will investigate the identity theft.'

'How long will the investigation take?'

'That's not something I can tell you, Tory. It depends on who the culprit is. If it's some random person, the investigation might be done quickly. If, on the other hand, it's an organised group, the investigation will be more complicated and take longer. Sometimes these crimes never get solved.'

'I just feel so vulnerable,' Tory bemoaned. 'I want my life back. With my money secure and with working cards, so I don't have to remember to carry enough cash all the time.'

'We'll do our best, Tory. I want to manage your expectations, though. These sorts of crimes often take many months, if not years, to finalise. I am sorry. I know that is not what you want to hear.'

'Oh my God, years. I can't put my life on hold for years. It's got to be sorted much sooner than that.'

'Can you call into the station on your way to work tomorrow? I'll be there early. Bring the letter notifying you of the credit card application and any paperwork from the bank. A statement or copy of your account details will be useful for us to investigate. I'll put together a few documents you might find helpful. There's a liaison officer I want to put you in touch with, in case you need more support.'

'We can do that. See you tomorrow.'

'And, Tory, don't worry too much. Trust me. The police will follow up all leads and get to the bottom of this, no matter how long it takes.'

'How long it takes is what I am now worried about, Detective,' Tory said as she ended the call.

CHAPTER 9

Brent parked the truck in a fifteen-minute parking space at the front of the police station. They didn't plan on being long. It was early, and Tory saw police in uniform and people in regular clothing walking into the station, many with a coffee cup in hand. A coffee cart on the nearby corner was doing a roaring trade. *It must be court day*, she thought. Next door at the courthouse, she saw a news crew setting up a camera. A reporter chatted to a woman in a suit, and a cleaner emptied a garbage bin next to the station entrance.

Detective Blunt walked from behind the front counter and greeted them with a smile. She was wearing dark pants and boots with a light-blue, striped shirt, her hair in a tight ponytail. Despite not wearing a uniform, to Tory, the detective still looked like a policewoman. She carried an air of no-nonsense authority that conveyed the impression she could get the job done.

'Good morning.'

'Morning, Detective,' Brent greeted her.

'Here are the documents you asked for,' Tory said, handing her the letter and account statements from the bank.

'Thank you, Tory,' she said, taking the documents and sliding them into the manila folder she was carrying.

'If you're not in a rush to get away, I would like you to meet Judy Winter. She is our police liaison with the cyber fraud squad in Sydney, and she will provide you with support.'

'What do you mean, from Sydney? Won't you be investigating anymore?' Tory asked.

'Cybercrime is complicated and requires more resources than we can provide locally. This type of crime often has national or international involvement, and so it makes sense there is one expert team investigating all the cybercrimes in the state. The cyber unit also liaises with other states and federal units.'

'So, now do we talk to you, or to someone in Sydney?' Brent asked.

'Still mostly me, although from time to time someone from the fraud unit may want to talk to you directly. You can talk to Judy, too. She's based locally and looks after all the stations in the local command,' Detective Blunt said as she turned towards a doorway, motioning with her hand for them to follow.

Brent and Tory looked at each other. Neither were happy their case was now being investigated from Sydney. Brent shrugged his shoulders, and they followed the detective to an office next to the main foyer, where a woman with grey curly hair, wearing large orange-rimmed glasses and a caftan dress sat at a computer.

'Good morning, Tory and Brent. I'm Judy,' she said, standing to shake their hands. Her colourful dress fell to its full length, reaching the floor, as she stood. She wore chunky orange earrings and a large stone-set ring on each hand. Her handshake was firm.

'Detective Blunt has filled me in on your case and the recent escalation. The fraud team in Sydney will investigate the ID theft. Unfortunately, there is a spate of ID fraud going on. Sadly, around twenty-five percent of people will experience some form of this theft in their lifetime. Some through company customer databases containing identity data being compromised; others, such as you, through having identity documents stolen.'

'Great, I've joined an enormous group,' Tory said as they all sat.

'Yes, and unfortunately, it comes at a huge inconvenience to the victim. Experts estimate it takes, on average, thirty-five non-consecutive hours of perseverance for an individual to restore their security.'

'Yeah, right. I'm well on the way to surpassing those hours,' Tory grumbled.

'I hope I can help you with that. There is a website with suggestions on how to secure your data. I'll show you the site, and we can discuss questions you may have,' Judy said.

'Sorry to interrupt,' Detective Blunt said, looking at Tory. 'I'll leave you now with Judy. Before you go, can you and Brent provide us with your fingerprints? When we find your car, we'll need them for elimination purposes, so we don't waste time and follow up on just the thieves' prints. The officer at the front desk can do them for you. It'll only take a minute.' Detective Blunt waved as she walked out the door. Tory froze for a second, blinked, then nodded her assent to the detective.

As the meeting wound up, Tory and Brent shared a look. They felt a bit more in control. There was a plan of action to get things back to normal. Judy was kind, and she reassured both Brent and Tory that they would get through this situation.

'Thank you for this information. You've been very helpful. I feel there is somewhere for me to start now, and get support from too, if we get stuck,' Tory said.

'You're welcome. Don't hesitate to get in contact if you have questions. Remember, while you'll have to work hard to clear the bad debts, the police are here to support you, and I can link you in with the team in Sydney if you need.'

Judy stood and directed the pair out the office door into the main foyer.

'Don't forget the fingerprints,' Judy said as she nodded goodbye.

The police officer at the front counter was speaking on the telephone.

'Brent, he looks busy. Let's come back and do the prints later,' Tory said.

'Don't be silly. He is hanging up the phone now. Let's see if he has time,' Brent said as he walked to the counter.

For elimination purposes, the detective said.

Tory's heart beat hard in her chest. She tried to put on a calm face. She didn't want to provide her prints. Standing in front of Brent and next to the officer, her instincts screamed, *Don't do this.* Her mind raced. No reason, sound or otherwise, came to her that would justify declining the prints. She was trapped.

'We will destroy the copies of your prints once we complete the investigation,' the officer said.

Confidently, Brent went first, rolling each finger on the electronic pad, then gestured for Tory to step up and do hers.

Damn, thought Tory as she stepped forward. *I hope they only look at the prints on the car for comparison.*

CHAPTER 10

Brent didn't know much about Tory's life before she moved to Aloma. Her past life looked very different to the life she now led. Her upbringing was traumatic, and Tory wasn't proud of many of the things she'd done. In fact, she felt deep shame. Tory feared if she revealed her past to anyone, they would think less of her, or worse, refuse to have anything to do with her.

Tory knew in her heart that if they'd known the full story, Brent would not have dated, let alone married, her. Nor would Frank have employed her. So, she kept her past a secret from everyone, and now she wanted it to stay that way.

As a kid, she led a troubled life. She never knew her father, and her mother could only be described as uncaring. By the time she went to high school, her mum was doing a daily hit of one upper or another.

Tory remembered one day, just before the Easter school holidays, that summed up her early life.

She walked home from school thinking about what she would do with herself for the next two weeks. Her home was in an area of town the locals called Govi Valley, on a street lined with commission homes: government-subsidised houses for those without means. Her house sat between two well-cared-for homes; the occupants mowed regularly and collected their junk mail. In contrast, her home was surrounded by knee-high weeds and shrubs dying of thirst.

She walked through the unlocked front door, letting the screen door bang behind her. In the lounge room, off the central passageway, the television blared on full volume. Not sure if she would find her mother strung out or high, she stuck her head in the doorway. The lounge looked as unloved as the front yard. Cracks riddled the walls, cobwebs hung from a single bare bulb, and the curtains sagged from their railing, their hems frayed or torn. Her mother lay on the ratty lounge, head back, eyes glazed, staring at the ceiling. Tory knew it was best not to disturb her and backed out quietly.

She smelt the kitchen before she got there. The house always stank. Nothing was ever cleaned. On the kitchen table, congealed remnants of food sat in takeaway containers. A rotten-meat smell came from the bin near the back door, and a pile of pizza boxes sat on the stovetop. Her mother must've had visitors today.

Only half the hotplates worked on the stove, which, as they didn't cook, didn't matter. Dirty dishes lay around on the table and piled in the sink. She always wondered why anyone bothered putting their dirty dish in the sink if they never planned on washing it anyway. She opened the door of the fridge, hoping the visitors had left something she could eat, but as usual, it was empty except for bottles of cola her mother drank with bourbon. She didn't bother looking for food in the cupboards. She would head out later tonight to the soup kitchen where she regularly ate her one good meal for the day. Her other source of food came from her mates, who understood what her life looked like and gave her food or cans of soft drink when they hung out.

She didn't trust her mother's friends, and to prevent unwanted guests roaming in on her, she slipped a chock under the bedroom door when she was in the room. Last week she put a lock on her bedroom door. A few days later, when she came home from school, the lock was broken. A crack ran down the door frame where a foot had kicked the door inwards. The few belongings she owned were tossed around the room, lying on the floor.

'Don' think you can hide shit from yer mum, you little bitch,' her mother screeched when she challenged her about the door.

Occasionally, in a fit of passion, Tory attempted to clean the house. With no vacuum cleaner, she swept the floors with an old broom. The house would stay tidy for a day or two, then, progressively, it would turn back to shit. Her room was the only one in the house to stay neat.

When she was on the edge of starving, or her clothes were falling apart or getting too small, she discovered she had particular skills useful for sneaking into homes to nick what she needed. She only took stuff she could use. Initially, she didn't sell what she stole. In these homes, she sometimes had the best meal she had eaten in months.

In year ten at school, she met Jordie. He stood a few centimetres shorter than her and had a wiry body. She thought he looked cute, and he made her laugh. Jordie was quick with his fists, regularly winning fights, and he liked to look out for her. Most of the kids in school avoided him. He also liked a challenge and leapt toward any promise of action. He quickly became her best friend, and she could depend on him. Together, they broke into homes. Life around Jordie was exciting, and for the first time, she sensed someone cared about her. Together, they began stealing things to sell. Jordie had contacts who gave them money for the nicked goods. Having money allowed her to walk into a shop and buy nice clothes. When she had money to shop, it made her feel normal, like everyone else.

In her bedroom, she made a hideaway for the new clothes, so her mother wouldn't sell them for drugs. Behind her wardrobe, she cut a hole in the plaster and stored her clothes, protected in plastic bags, in the cavity. She then pushed the wardrobe back against the wall to hide the hole. Her mother was generally too wasted to notice when she wore new clothes. By the time she was sixteen, she and Jordie broke into homes every week. She kept a stash of cash hidden in a zip-lock bag behind the unused compost bin in the backyard. Her mother never found either hiding spot.

One day, as she and Jordie snuck out of a house, she looked up to see two police officers standing, hands on hips, looking at her. Their break-in had triggered a silent alarm.

'You two are under arrest.'

The police officer snapped handcuffs over her wrists, and the link ratcheted closed, the cold metal of the cuffs warming quickly to her skin temperature. The officers marched them to the police car. One pushed her head down as he manoeuvred her into the backseat, next to Jordie.

Jordie looked straight ahead. Out of the corner of his mouth, he mumbled, 'Don't say nuffin.'

She nodded and sat in silence as they drove.

The police car pulled up at the station, where they had their fingerprints taken. The police charged her with breaking and entering and theft. Charges they later dropped when her circumstances became obvious. When the police attended her home, they were unimpressed by the reception they received from her mother, and fortunately, they gave her a second chance. The police warned her any further break-ins would mean she might go to jail.

'Your fingerprints will stay on file for a while, so don't reoffend.'

She was seventeen then, a minor. Tory now anxiously hoped, seven years later, those prints were destroyed.

CHAPTER 11

'Brent, that's the fifth time I've called a mother from childcare to pick up Laura and bring her home,' Tory moaned. 'I miss my little Honda. I'm sick of imposing on everyone. Aloma is lovely, but absolutely hopeless for public transport.'

Tory loved living in Aloma. The city was small but provided all the facilities their young family needed, and it was also just far enough away from where Brent's parents lived to allow a buffer from daily interference by his mother.

'Tors, I am not sure what else we can do. It won't be forever. The insurance will come through in a few weeks.'

'Can we buy a car without waiting for the insurance? Get a loan or something?'

* * *

Tory's lack of a car worried Brent, too. He knew he was pushing the love at work. Every day this week, he'd arrived late to work so he could drop Laura at school first, and at the other end of the day, he found himself driving from one place to the next, running the errands Tory normally handled. Although Tory was welcome to use his truck after hours, with all his tools in the back, they didn't want to leave the truck unattended in supermarkets or other public spaces for too long in case someone decided to break in and steal his work gear.

Brent admitted to himself he enjoyed the extra time with Laura in the mornings, but he found juggling everything complicated and somewhat exhausting, especially on the evenings he had footy training. He enjoyed training, and he didn't want to feel guilty about going. He appreciated his mum and other parents helping care for Laura after school when needed, but wondered how long it would be before they, too, found the now-regular lending a hand an inconvenience.

'Let's do the sums tonight and see what's possible. I'll have a squiz on the car sales web pages and see what they have. I'll ask around. Maybe one of the boys will know someone who is trying to sell their car,' Brent said.

'Thanks, babe. It'd be good to get back to a normal life, of sorts.'

* * *

The next day, after work, Tory walked the last block towards her house, grateful for the lift from her workmate. The afternoon was lovely, lightening her step. As the sun dropped behind the trees, the air became pleasantly cool. Bright red parakeets greeted her, flying and swooping playfully on lawns as she walked by.

As she reached her gateway, she spotted a large box on the doorstep.

A thrill of excitement buzzed her body. It always felt a little like Christmas when parcels arrived. The box covered most of the doormat below the front door. Tory put her handbag on the porch, gripped the edge of the box, and, while pressing her knee against the side of the box, shoved it off the mat to one side so she could open the front door. Her grin grew wide as she read her name on the address label. The box was awkward to manoeuvre, so she shuffled it sideways through the front door and slid it along the passageway to the kitchen.

Tory grunted with exertion as she heaved the box up onto the kitchen bench. She quickly tore off the packing tape and opened the top. On tiptoes, she peered inside. It was a KitchenAid complete with a full set of attachments. Tory let out a cry of delight. Only a few months ago, while shopping with Brent, she'd pointed out this appliance.

'Babe, this would make cooking a dream,' Tory said, batting her eyelids at him.

'Not at that price,' Brent scoffed. 'I'll buy you one when we win the lotto.'

How did he afford this? Tory wondered, stunned. She hummed a happy tune as she set the contents onto the bench.

She heard his truck arrive home. He'd gone to pick up Laura from one of the mothers' homes.

Tory met them at the door and flung her arms around Brent.

'Thank you, babe, thank you so much. I can't believe you bought it for me. It's not even my birthday. Did you get a bonus from work you didn't tell me about?'

'Whoa, Tory, slow down. What are you talking about?' Brent said, laughing at her excitement.

'Mummy, Mummy, what did you get? Show me,' Laura said.

She jumped up and down on the spot.

'Yes, show us,' Brent said as he followed Tory to the kitchen.

Tory waved her hand across the Kitchen Aid set up on the bench.

'I love the red colour. I'm going to cook a cake tonight. I can't wait to use it.'

'Tors,' Brent said, his tone cautious. 'I didn't order this.'

'But it's what I wanted … how … what do you mean? Oh no,' Tory said as realisation hit her. 'The fraud. Oh damn, not again, not this.' Tory's face crumpled with disappointment.

'Let's see if we can figure out who ordered it and how they paid for it. We'll have to contact Detective Blunt and the bank again.'

'I don't suppose I can use it?' Tory asked, looking at the Kitchen Aid with disappointment as Brent, his face scowling, packed the components back in the box.

'Tors, you have to be more careful. This sort of thing could end up financially hurting us. Don't touch anything delivered here until you know for sure one of us bought it. We have to return this.'

His words stung Tory. This afternoon, she had gone from thinking Brent was loving and generous to being chastised by him.

'Sure. I'll check the bank statements to see if money came from one of our accounts,' Tory said, her voice a whisper as she blinked back tears.

Tory logged onto the home computer in the dining room and scrolled through the bank accounts.

'Nothing from our accounts, Brent,' Tory mumbled, not looking up, still hurting from his earlier words.

'Which means they probably have a credit card in your name, one we don't know about, and they forgot to change the postal address, or maybe they plan to change it now the account is operational. We need to call Detective Blunt so she can find and cancel the card.'

Fear seeped through Tory. Knowing someone had a credit card in her name, spending money, which the card company would expect her to repay, made her feel vulnerable. Hell, what if the thieves spent lots of money, and the card company refused to believe the fraud against Tory? Would she have to pay? They might lose all their savings and still be in debt. A tension headache was forming behind her eyes.

Both the bank and Detective Blunt took Tory's calls, noting the delivery.

Tory planned to ask the detective about the debt the criminals incurred in her name and what would happen about repaying the debt, but Detective Blunt was rushed and couldn't talk for long. She promised to get back to Tory as soon as she could. The person at the bank asked Tory to call tomorrow during working hours to follow up further.

'In the meantime, I recommend you contact the store that sent the Kitchen Aid. They should have the purchase details and might tell you how the goods were paid for. If it was by credit card, they may tell you which institution the card came from.'

As she disconnected the call, Tory sighed. She was beginning to feel like Sisyphus. Weary, she turned to look for the invoice attached to the delivery.

CHAPTER 12

At her work desk the following day, Tory looked around for Frank. She needed to call the bank but didn't want him to see her taking more personal time. Frank had been understanding about the theft, but Tory noticed his growing impatience when she asked for time to sort things out with the bank or for more flexibility with work hours around the availability of lifts home after work.

Tory watched Frank walk out the back door, toward the employee car park. She assumed he was heading out and leant over to pick up her handbag from next to her desk. She fished out her phone and dialled the bank. As it rang, she kept an eye on the back door in case he walked back in. It took a few minutes of pressing buttons to get through the automated bank concierge and talk to a person. Then she was passed on to another person, then another, until finally, she spoke to someone who was familiar with her story.

'Your file notes state you called yesterday evening. This bank is not involved in the transaction, from what I can tell.'

'I checked my accounts but couldn't see any withdrawals, so that must mean there is a credit card or something in my name.'

'Tory, there are a number of possibilities. Someone may have a credit card in your name. The card could've come from a number of different institutions, not necessarily a bank. It could also mean there may be a loan in your name, and they are paying for things from the loan.'

'Oh God, no. Can't you do something to stop this from happening?' Tory pleaded.

'I'm sorry, Tory. This is a matter for the police, not the bank as such. The usual bank security is on your accounts. Unfortunately, I can't do anything about what other institutions do with your details. It might be worth you doing another credit check on yourself to see if you can find any other irregularity.'

'Well, thanks anyway. I hope the police can help.'

She disconnected the call, rested her head in her hands, and quietly moaned.

'Hey, girlfriend, what's the matter?' Carolyn said, standing at the doorway. 'Why the sad face?'

'Oh, Caro, this credit nightmare is never going to go away. It's the gift that keeps on giving, and it just gets worse. The bank told me to do another credit check to find out if there are any other loans in my name, ones we didn't find in the first check. KitchenAids could be getting delivered to hundreds of people under my name!'

'Well, I'm disappointed I haven't received one yet,' Carolyn said with a quick smile. 'Hang in there, girlfriend. Focus on doing things one step at a time, as you need to.'

Good advice, Tory understood, but her financial security was on the line, and that scared her.

Later, at lunch time, Tory sat with Carolyn and a few others in the staff kitchen. As she unwrapped her sandwich, her mobile rang. She answered the phone, glancing at the screen and noting no caller ID was displayed.

'Hello.'

'Hi. Is this Tory Packenham?'

'Sure is. Who is this?'

'I am from Support Kids Australia. Your pledge of a one-hundred-dollar donation has bounced. Can you please provide another credit card to make the payment?'

'What donation? I haven't donated to you.'

'Well, I'm sorry. There is a commitment notice in front of me, with a credit card in your name. The card was just rejected, so I am trying to reconcile the debt.'

'It's not a bad debt; it's fraud!' Tory screamed as she ended the call and slammed her phone on the table. She looked up to see five concerned faces staring at her and burst into tears. Carolyn leant forward and put her arms around Tory in a gentle hug. Over the top of Tory's head, she nodded to the others, who, looking mortified, grabbed their lunches and snuck out.

'Shh. It's okay, girlfriend. We are here for you.' Carolyn rubbed Tory's back.

'I am so humiliated,' Tory sobbed to Carolyn. 'In front of the crew, too. They heard about me not paying *a charity*, of all things. What must they think of me? And to top it off, here I am crying. Damn it. Just bloody damn it!'

Carolyn handed her a tissue.

'They know about the credit card theft. No one thinks badly

of you. Stay strong, girlfriend. It will sort itself out. You'll see.' Carolyn gave her another reassuring hug.

* * *

When Tory arrived home that evening, she shared with Brent the events of her disastrous day. After Laura went to bed, they sat together at their computer to run the credit check.

'It seems crazy I am doing this again,' Tory said. 'It was only a few weeks ago I ran the first one.'

'Oh well, we need to be sure, I suppose.'

Tory typed in her details and turned to Brent.

'Brent, give me your credit card details. I need to pay for this, and, of course, *I* don't have any cards.'

Brent looked at her. 'Of course, I'll give them to you. Just ask nicely. No need to be narky with me.' He stood and walked from the room.

Oh crap, thought Tory.

The tension frustrated her. She sounded grumpy all the time.

She hit 'enter' to finalise the credit check and was notified it should be back in a day or two. Tory sat back and sighed. She felt another headache developing. If only she could have a do-over for today, she would handle things better. She stood wearily and looked around for Brent so she could apologise.

* * *

'Frank, can I take the afternoon off, please? More stuff has happened with the credit card theft, and Brent wants us to go to the bank in person. We keep getting the runaround on the phone.'

'Tory, I suppose if you must, you can. Please sort this out soon. I don't want this distraction to go on any longer.'

'Thanks, Frank. Hopefully, things will get sorted soon.'

Brent picked Tory up from work in the early afternoon, and they drove to the bank to meet with their 'personal banker'.

'Brent and Tory, I understand you want this resolved, but until the police find the culprit, and even if they do, you will need to keep vigilant and get onto any suspicious transaction as soon as you discover it. It might take months to catch up with all the fraud instigated in the first few weeks of the theft. It really is a police matter, not something the bank can resolve.'

'So, there is nothing you can do?' Brent asked.

'We maintain our usual security on your accounts. You've set up the SMS alert for any payments, so you can keep on top of anything from this bank. Beyond that, no, there is nothing else we can do.'

As they left the bank, Tory turned to Brent.

'Well, that wasn't very satisfying. I don't think our visit resolved the situation at all. I feel we're hanging on, waiting for the thieves to do the next thing so we can stop them. It's as if we're in a B-grade movie, playing catch-up all the time.'

'I agree. I wish I could get my hands on them. I'd wring their necks. I've missed half a day of work and don't think we are any better off.'

'I am sorry, Brent. I know it's my cards. I'm glad you came with me today.'

'No worries, Tors. It's just incredibly frustrating.'

Arriving home, Tory logged onto the computer and checked her emails.

'Brent, the credit check is back,' she called out. 'Oh shit,' she exclaimed, looking at the screen. 'There are six cards now in my name, all from different institutions.'

'What the …' Brent rushed into the room. 'Okay, we need to call all the businesses and cancel those cards, straight away.'

They chose three organisations each and started calling.

Two hours later, they were done.

'I am so exhausted,' Tory said, sitting back in her chair.

'Me too. I can't count how many times I had to say, "My wife did not apply for this card, her details were stolen," and give them the police incident number. I don't have much more left in me,' Brent said as he flopped down on a seat next to Tory.

'How about you go pick up Laura, and I will be chef tonight? A bottle of wine with dinner might help us relax. Is that okay?' Tory asked.

'Sounds like a plan. Be back soon,' Brent said, grabbing his car keys off the bench and heading to the garage.

Before preparing dinner, Tory checked their mailbox, a task she now approached with dread. She feared what might arrive next. Last week, several credit card payment notices arrived. Each notice required long follow-up phone calls with the card companies. Most didn't believe her when she told them she hadn't spent the money and the card was not hers. One company threatened to send debt collectors to the house.

After that particular call, Tory hung up in a cold sweat. She was fearful of what the debt collectors might do. Brent and Tory were unsure if they should pay some of the accounts to get the debt collectors off their backs or to fight. Brent was worried about their finances.

'There are the savings for the house deposit, but I don't want to dip into that. On the other hand, I am worried about someone harassing you,' he told her.

'I haven't been harassed too much yet. Let's see if we can continue to convince agencies the cards are the result of fraudulent applications,' Tory said. 'I don't want to lose any of our savings either. We can't access the money in the fixed deposit account, anyway.'

CHAPTER 13

Tory woke with a yawn late Saturday morning after a sleep disturbed by dreams. As she walked into the kitchen, she was assaulted by a five-year-old running towards her, arms held out wide. Laura leapt into her arms.

'Morning, Mummy. You smell nice.'

'Morning, darling. You are very cuddly this morning.' Tory kissed her on the neck.

'Daddy is looking for new cars for us. Look,' Laura said. Her raised finger pointed toward Brent, who was sitting at the computer, searching the online car sales pages.

'Oh, and has Daddy found us a car?' Tory asked. She smiled at Brent.

'There are a few that might be good. None for the insurance money, though. We're short about half of the asking price. We'll need to borrow money,' Brent said.

'Who will loan us money while we have the credit card fraud issue?' asked Tory.

'Well, I was thinking, your work has a staff loan scheme for big-ticket items. It might be worth asking. They offer cheaper interest rates, and as an employee, they know you are good for it.'

'Good idea. I hadn't considered a work loan. I'll ask on Monday. They might loan us the full amount for the car upfront with the expectation we can pay back the first $8,600 as soon as the car insurance money is paid. Show me the ones you selected,' Tory said, sitting next to Brent, with Laura perched on her knee, staring intently at the cars on the screen.

After a while, Brent raised his arms and stretched away from the computer. 'Okay, we've seen most of them. Let's go for a test drive,' he said.

'I'll grab my bag. This is fun. It's exciting looking for a new car.'

'Munchkin, would it be okay if Caro came with us, to watch you while Mum and Dad test drive the cars?' Brent said, patting Laura on the head.

'Yay. Yes, Caro can come with us, please,' Laura said. She jumped on the spot with excitement. 'But I need to sit in the car to test it for me,' she said, eyeing Brent, challenging him to say otherwise.

'Of course,' Brent said, laughing. 'Tors, can you call Caro to ask if she can come with us?'

* * *

The group arrived back home from the car yards. Tory walked into the house, followed by Carolyn, Brent, and Laura.

'Who's up for a coffee?' Tory asked as she switched on the kettle.

The adults nodded. Laura stepped to the fridge, lifted out a milk carton, and poured herself a glass. After taking a sip of milk, she looked at Brent and Tory.

'I liked the red one. It had a nice middle bench for my dolls.'

'Yes, Laura, the red one was nice, although I reckon the best car was the white one at the first car yard we visited. It had the least kilometres on it, and it was smooth to drive. There was plenty of room in the back for you, too, Munchkin,' Brent said.

'It was also the right price,' Tory said.

'Mmm, okay. Let's go get it, then,' Laura said.

'We need to get the loan approved first,' Tory said, laughing. 'Hopefully, Frank can do it quickly. I would hate for the car to sell to someone else,' she said, looking at Carolyn, who nodded back.

* * *

After another juggle of rides, Tory arrived at work on Monday a fraction before clock-on time. She filled out the paperwork for the loan on the staff webpage and hit the 'submit' button. Then she walked by Frank's office and poked her head inside the door.

'Hi, Frank.'

'Tory, how are you? How's your weekend?'

'Good, thanks. I just wanted to give you a heads-up. I've submitted a staff loan application to buy a car. It doesn't seem like the police will find my stolen one anytime soon. I'll be able to pay out half the loan in the first few weeks as soon as the insurance pays.'

'Thanks for telling me, Tory. I'll review it as soon as I can. It will take a few days, though. I should be able to get back to you by late Wednesday.'

'Thanks, Frank,' Tory said as she walked back to her desk. She was getting excited thinking about the new car.

* * *

It was footy training night again, and Brent's mother picked up Laura after school. They were in the kitchen when Tory arrived home.

'Hi, Gail. Thanks for picking up Laura again.'

'No problem. I like spending time with her, and to be honest, it also gets me out of the house, away from Gordon. Sometimes he drives me mad with all his pottering.'

I wonder who gets driven mad more, Gail or Gordon?

'Well, we appreciate it, Gail, and for putting a casserole on too. I'm not sure what we would've eaten tonight otherwise.'

'You must eat properly, especially Brent, with all his physical work. He has to keep up his strength, and Laura needs her nutrition.'

Tory flinched.

Why can't she just do something nice and not lord it over me?

'When do you think you might get a replacement car, so you can pick up Laura? Not that I mind picking her up. It's just a bit out of my way, so I'm wondering how long I need to be doing this?' Gail queried as she picked up her handbag and keys from the kitchen bench.

'Hopefully, my loan application will come through in the next few days, and we probably can get the new car by the end of the week. Fingers crossed.'

'That would be ideal. Give Grandma a kiss, Laura. I am going home now.'

Laura looked up from the kitchen table where she was drawing.

'Bye, Grandma. See you later.' She blew an air kiss and lowered her head back down, refocusing on her drawing.

'See you, Gail,' Tory said. She waved as Gail got into her car. *Wicked witch.*

Tory returned inside and sat next to her daughter.

'How was your day, Laura? Was it fun at school?'

'It was alright, Mummy. Will pushed Greta over at lunchtime, and she skun her knee, and he made her cry. The teacher told Will to apologise and sent him inside early from lunch.'

'Oh dear, I hope Greta is alright now.'

'Yes, she is good. Mummy, do I have to brush my hair a hundred times every night like Grandma told me? It takes too long, and I want to play,' Laura asked.

Tory sighed. 'No, just as long as your hair is neat, a quick brush is fine,' she replied, giving Laura a lingering hug.

* * *

Tory was sitting at her desk, following up accounts, when she looked up to see Frank walking past. He paused and spoke to her.

'Tory, can you come to my office, please?'

'Sure,' Tory said. Frank walked with determination, a serious look on his face, one she couldn't read. Tory felt a sense of unease as she followed him to his office.

'Shut the door, please,' Frank directed as she entered the office space. He sat behind his desk, not asking her to take a seat. Suddenly, Tory was fearful.

'Tory, I don't quite know how to say this. To say I am stunned is an understatement,' Frank said, looking at Tory.

Tory blinked at him, her forehead creasing.

'What's wrong?'

Frank's face reddened. Tory wasn't sure if it was in anger or embarrassment.

'Your checks for the loan came back. Your credit rating score is only three hundred and twenty. There are bad debts everywhere. You can't have bad debts. You are our credit manager, for goodness' sake!' he said, waving his hands in the air.

'What are you talking about?' Tory said. 'There can't be a bad credit rating. I've always paid my debts. I only have one loan at the moment, for some investments, and I've never missed a payment. There have been some cards I had to cancel as part of the fraud, but no bad debts I'm aware of.'

'That's not what's on the credit register. I am truly shocked, Tory. We can't employ someone in your job who can't manage funds,' Frank said, his face darkening.

'I don't understand the rating. It must be a mistake,' Tory begged, blindsided by the overt threat to her job.

'It doesn't look like a mistake. It's all here.' Frank indicated towards his computer.

'Let me see the rating, please.'

Frank turned the computer screen toward her, the rating alert clear on the screen.

'Maybe there are two Tory Packenhams?' she said, desperately trying to give some explanation. 'It can't be me.'

'I checked every detail, birth date, address, and it looks like you.'

'Frank, you're aware my identity's been stolen. Those debts can't be mine. It's taking ages to sort out,' Tory said, the pitch of her voice rising in distress.

'Well, I hope it's just related to the current situation. As it is, however, the company can't approve your loan,' Frank said. He stood and crossed his arms, standing in front of Tory. 'You need to sort this out immediately. It's not good, especially for someone in your position.'

Their conversation hit Tory like a punch to the guts. There was no way she and Brent were going to get a loan from anyone to get a car, and now Frank was looking at her with suspicion. It hurt. She wanted Frank to trust her, just as he always had. Tears welled in her eyes. She was determined not to cry. God, even worse, she might lose her job over this.

'I'm trying to sort it. I'm sorry. I just can't think of what else to do. I'll talk to the police again. Thanks for telling me,' Tory mumbled. She nearly stumbled in her haste to turn and leave his office.

Visibly upset, Tory headed back to her desk, past Carolyn, who looked up at her with concern and offered a sympathetic nod when she caught her eye. Tory acknowledged her with a returned nod, lips pursed, as she turned to her desk and sat.

Tory picked up her mobile and called Brent. The phone rang, then went to voicemail. 'Brent, the loan got knocked back. My credit rating is now bad. I'm not sure what to do next. Talk tonight.' She disconnected the call and burst into tears.

CHAPTER 14

'Tory, wake up. Are you alright?' Tory opened her eyes to see Brent leaning over her. She'd fallen asleep on the couch waiting for Brent to come home. She was exhausted.

'I had the most awful dream. Financially, things were completely out of control. It felt so real. I'm completely shattered.'

'It didn't have anything to do with this?' Brent said as he held out an opened letter of demand addressed to Tory. 'They are threatening to take you to court for nonpayment.'

A short time later, Tory sipped on the tea Brent made for her as they sat side by side at their computer. Fully awake now, she felt better.

'Tors, I was talking to one of the guys at work, and he suggested you should put a block freeze on your credit use. The freeze means when organisations do a credit rating check, and they see a block, they won't loan you any money. Since a car loan is now out of the question, we should activate the block so no one else can access credit in your name.'

'Why didn't the guys at the bank tell me to do that at the beginning? Why am I only finding out about this now?'

Brent shrugged his shoulders.

'It means you can't get a loan while the block is on. Perhaps they knew we were looking at getting a home loan sometime? Let's log on and check how hard it is to do.'

The process turned out to be pretty simple, and Tory activated the block in less than half an hour.

'Let's hope things will settle down now,' Brent said.

'Brent, should you do a credit check on your finances?'

'Maybe, I guess? We haven't applied for any loans jointly, so it should be okay, but just to be sure, I'll do one.'

'It's a shame you still have the loan outstanding on your truck, or you could have applied for a loan for my car.'

'Sure, but I do, and my salary isn't high enough to pay off both loans without factoring in your income, which now they won't do,' Brent said.

'What are we going to do, Brent?' Tory's stomach was in knots. She was sure an ulcer was developing.

'Don't worry. Something will come up. Worst case, we look for a cheaper car, one your insurance payout will cover. It should only be a week or two before the payout gets approved,' Brent said. He gave Tory a hug.

Tory relaxed a little in the warmth of his arms. Brent always made her feel safe.

Suddenly, Tory's mobile phone rang. She looked at the screen. No caller ID showed.

'No ID. Should I answer it?' Tory said, holding the phone towards Brent. 'I guess I'd better, in case it's important.' She brought the phone up to her ear.

'Hello.'

'Hello, Tory. It's Detective Blunt.'

Tory breathed out with relief. She'd been expecting a debt collector or scammer.

'Oh, hi. Has something happened? Do you have any updates for me?'

'Sorry, Tory. No recent developments, I am afraid. I'm calling to tell you we are still working as hard as we can to investigate. Your car still hasn't been located.'

'What about the ID fraud? Have you found out who is responsible for that?'

'No. The guys from the Sydney fraud office called earlier today to tell me they believe your details may have been sent overseas, making it very difficult to trace. An international team is working on a number of ID fraud cases linked to international syndicates.'

'Well, I am sorry,' Tory exploded. 'That is just not good enough! I now have a bad credit rating, and my boss is starting to doubt my ability to be his credit manager. I could even lose my job!'

'We're trying very hard, Tory. The team is putting lots of hours into it. The fraud we are dealing with is complex.'

'Why didn't you tell me to block freeze my credit? It's taken me almost three weeks to find out I can freeze my credit. You should've told me,' Tory yelled.

'Calm down, Tory, please. Information on credit freezing was on one of the brochures you were given when we first met. It's an option, but it means you can't get a loan or even a new credit card while the freeze is on. I can't tell you what you should do here, Tory,' Detective Blunt said in a concerned tone.

'I don't remember seeing it. I was probably too stressed about my family being a victim of *aggravated* burglary,' said Tory. She felt simultaneously angry and defeated.

'Tory, I will be in contact as soon as any new information comes to light. Stay on top of your finances, work with your bank. Understand there are a number of other people in the same situation as you with the ID theft, and the team in Sydney is working day and night to find and apprehend the criminals.'

Tory was contrite for yelling at the detective.

'Okay, sorry for yelling. I am so incredibly frustrated. Hopefully, there will be some sort of resolution soon.'

'No worries. Talk soon,' the detective replied and ended the call.

'Phew, that was intense. Come here,' Brent said, pulling Tory into the comfort of his arms.

* * *

Tory and Carolyn sat together, alone in the work tearoom, eating lunch. Tory finished telling Carolyn about her call with the detective the previous night.

'I may have overdone it a tad. I don't know if Detective Blunt will like me much from now on. I was pretty harsh.'

'Girlfriend, no one dislikes you. I am sure she understands the pressure you are under and how vulnerable that makes you. Of course, you got exasperated. It probably happens all the time.'

'That's not an excuse for me yelling at the poor woman. I am so desperate at the moment. I want the whole thing to go away. Now I can't get the car loan, I'll have to wait a week or two for the insurance, and keep juggling rides and asking favours. I am so over everything,' Tory groaned.

'Hey. I just had a thought,' Carolyn said. Her voice rose with excitement. 'If it still goes, you can use Nan's car.'

'Didn't you get rid of it?'

'No. I was going to sell it. I remember telling you that, but when it came time, I couldn't bring myself to do it. It's been sitting in the garage unused since she went into the home. After six months, the battery is probably flat at least.'

'Oh, Caro, that would be fantastic! Can I come home after work with you to see if we can get it to start?' Tory asked, her eyes wide and hopeful.

'Of course. It's pretty old. I think Nan bought it new when she was sixty-two or three,' Carolyn said. 'The car might be thirty or forty years old.'

'I don't care how old it is, as long as it goes. Anything would be good at this point. Thank you so much.'

'I'm sorry I didn't think of it before. I just assumed you would buy another car. I hope it's still drivable.'

Four hours later, Tory laughed at the stunned look on Brent's face as she drove the dorky-looking, bright-orange Mazda3 into their driveway.

'Bloody hell, what the heck's that?' Brent said, smiling.

'Caro's nan's car. All it needed was a jumpstart, and now the engine's running fine. It's not pretty, but it goes, and I now have wheels!' Tory couldn't wipe the smile off her face.

CHAPTER 15

Tory and Brent agreed to meet the detectives at the police station. Tory was reluctant to go. She hated those places and thought Detective Blunt had sounded unusually terse when they spoke on the phone early that morning.

'Hi, Tory. I need to speak to you and Brent at the station today, as soon as you can, please.'

'Has something happened? Can you just tell me now?' Tory asked.

'No, we need to see you both.'

How odd.

When she told Brent, he raised his eyebrows.

'She wouldn't tell you anything?'

Tory shook her head.

Brent shrugged his shoulders. 'Something must've happened.'

Tory and Brent had been working with the two detectives for the past three weeks, and neither had insisted they come to the station before today. Updates on the phone were usually fine, or the detectives would come to them. Maybe there had been a breakthrough in the robbery investigation? Still, she found Detective

Blunt's tone troubling. She sounded formal and, if Tory was frank, pissed. In the past, the detective had been supportive toward Tory. She wondered what could be wrong.

They dropped Laura at school, and after watching her run off to play, Brent turned the wheel of his truck, did a U-turn, and drove them back toward the police station. He pulled up at the kerb in front of the station.

Tory reached out and held Brent's hand as they skirted the bollards protecting the building against any crazed drivers intent on revenge and walked toward the station entrance. The double glass doors slid open, and they stepped inside to the main waiting room. The noise of the traffic, silenced by the closing doors, morphed into the quiet hum of activity. Sound radiated from the room beyond where they were standing.

Tory stopped, and her hand let go of Brent's as he walked on to the counter. Tory turned her head and looked around the station. The stark white walls exuded a sense of sterility, blandness. Despite the bright posters promoting safety messages dotted around the walls, the room lacked personality. The brightness of the fluorescent lights unnerved her. Her skin prickled, and she dabbed at the perspiration on her top lip.

Tory stepped beside Brent at the long counter; she could sense his warmth, his steady breathing. He strained his neck, trying to look behind the Perspex barrier from where sounds of talking wafted. Police on phones, doing what they do, she supposed.

Looking behind her, she saw a drug-thin young man in faded, torn jeans and a black singlet, covered in tattoos, sitting, concentrating on his phone. An unwashed smell came from his direction.

He's probably been in those clothes for days, Tory thought, her nose wrinkling.

'Tory and Brent Packenham, here to see Detective Blunt,' Brent announced to the officer at the front.

Moments later, Detective Blunt, with a stern look on her face, walked through a door to the side of the counter and motioned for them to follow her. They were led into a small meeting room. The room was devoid of warmth. It contained a Laminex table with six plastic chairs around it. A telephone, with several cables protruding, sat on one end of the table. Tory thought they were probably used to connect a computer for a videoconference or something similar. The only window, long and thin, ran at shoulder height across the inside wall. The bare walls were a pale blue.

Calming colours, Tory thought. She looked down and saw that her hands were shaking.

Detective Morgan, already sitting, motioned for them to take a seat.

Neither detective smiled, nor made welcoming small talk.

Brent looked at Tory, his face puzzled; this seemed so formal compared to the previous way the detectives interacted with them.

Detective Blunt remained standing, then leaned her tall frame forward, resting her hand on the table, facing them. She eyeballed Tory and asked, 'Does the name Pricilla Lisa-Maree Banes mean anything to either of you?'

'Not to me,' Brent said, frowning in confusion.

An empty silence followed. Everyone looked at Tory, waiting for her response. She felt like the stark walls of the room were pulsing. Colour drained from her face. She knew what she said next would impact her marriage. She was scared of how Brent would react. Could he forgive her lies? For a split second, Tory considered just saying no. To pretend the name meant nothing to her. She could make it go away by saying nothing. Then a look into the eyes of the detectives told her they knew. They would know she was lying. Tory hesitated, her face pale. She shut her eyes and hung her head.

'It's a name from long ago,' she whispered.

CHAPTER 16

Tory hung her head. Silence filled the interview room. She took a long, deep, shaky breath.

'What the heck, Tory? What are you talking about?' Brent said. He looked at her, his face creased with confusion.

Both detectives and Brent stared at her, waiting for her to say something. Tory felt chilled. Her body gave an involuntary shiver. She felt small. She wished she could make herself even smaller, small enough to disappear. They expected an explanation. Tension filled the air. There would be no hiding from this, not this time. She took another deep breath.

'It's something from when I was a teenager. I had a different name. It's got nothing to do with the robbery or the ID fraud,' Tory whispered, not looking at anyone, eyes focused on the table in front of her.

'Regardless, Tory, you haven't been completely honest with us, have you?' Detective Blunt said, her lips thin, her eyebrows joined in a frown.

'Honest with you?' Brent said loudly. 'I married her and didn't know she had another name!'

Miserable, Tory looked at Brent. Her heart ached. Her life had sunk to a new low point. It was a nightmare. Everything was going wrong.

'I was running away from someone who was dangerous, who wanted to hurt me. I didn't want them to find me, so I changed my name,' Tory said, her words trembling.

'There are no reports on you by either name. No violence, or AVOs,' Detective Morgan said, clearly sceptical of her story. 'No indication of you being at risk of violence.'

'I was a kid. My life was, well, it was different. I didn't report something that happened. No one would've believed me. No one would've kept me safe, so I ran away,' Tory pleaded.

'How come you never told me this?' Brent said. He looked confused and hurt. In front of the police, he seemed unsure how to respond. His face fell as if his world had crashed around him.

'I was scared. I hoped I might've left the past behind and could simply share the future with you. I don't know. I'm sorry,' Tory said, her shoulders slumped.

'I need to get out of here,' Brent said as he looked at the detectives. 'Is there anything else you need from us? Can we go?'

'That's all for now. We'll be in contact soon,' Detective Blunt said, eyeing Tory.

Tory saw she was pissed off with her. Worse, she had never seen Brent look more upset and angry. She was terrified. What would happen now?

Brent pushed up from his chair. He stormed from the meeting room and out the station front doors. Tory followed, stumbling in her effort to catch up with him.

'Brent, Brent, slow down, slow down. Please wait,' she called.

He jumped into the truck, slamming the door behind him. Tory was a few seconds behind. She climbed into the passenger side and looked at him. Brent looked back at her, his face a masked mystery. Tory was terrified of what might be going through his mind.

They sat silently in the truck. Brent gripped the steering wheel so tight his knuckles turned white. He stayed silent, unable to speak. She didn't blame him for being upset. The revelation floored him. He hadn't spoken a word to her since the initial outburst at the police station. Tory was afraid everything she had worked for would now be lost. Brent might leave her.

Tory burst into tears.

* * *

An hour ago, the house break-in was all Brent had to worry about. Now he felt he didn't know anything anymore. They'd prided themselves on their honesty with each other, or so he'd thought.

His Tory, a different name, fearing for her life?

What the heck? Why hadn't she told him? What other secrets did she hold?

Brent eyed Tory. He didn't reach out to comfort her. His hands stayed clutching the steering wheel. His heart raced in anger, and he felt consumed by a feeling of betrayal. Was their marriage a sham? Right now, nothing made sense to him.

'Okay, tell me. Tell me what's going on, Tory. I don't understand. You're another person?'

* * *

What could she tell him? He deserved the truth, but the truth might mean he would leave her.

'Oh, Brent, I am so sorry,' she sobbed. 'It's a long story. Can we please go somewhere quiet, not this car park, and I will tell you everything.'

'Everything should've been said years ago,' Brent said in anger as he slammed the truck in reverse and screeched out of the car park.

He drove to the nearby lake, parked the car so they overlooked the water, lowered the windows, and turned to her.

'Okay, your turn. Tell me everything.'

'I did stuff when I was young, not good things. I ended up running for my life, and that's when I changed my name. So the man chasing me wouldn't find me.'

'Yeah, you said that at the station. You've got to tell me everything, Tors,' Brent said, his lips pursed.

'I grew up in the slums of inland Port Macquarie. I wasn't lucky enough to experience the nice family upbringing you did. My mother mostly didn't work and lived on welfare. She sometimes did "favours" for men for cash. We were dead broke. I never had any money. In primary school, my brother, Sam, and I barely had food, let alone clothes to wear to school. When I got to high school, I found a good mate, Jorden. Jordie and I shoplifted, mostly to get things Mum didn't buy for me, things I needed, essentials. Then we moved to nicking stuff to sell. We wagged school a few days most weeks, when we would scope out what to nick. Cash was the holy grail, but we would take anything. Jordie knew how to sell the stuff we stole, and we always went halves in the cash. I mostly used the money to buy food and smokes.

Clothes we usually nicked. Sam used to protect me a bit, at home, from Mum's rants.'

'She beat you?' Brent asked.

'Not really. Sam stood interference when she accused me of things, not very rational things, but hurtful for a kid. Anyway, the day after my thirteenth birthday, Sam left home. He didn't say goodbye, just walked out. He came back the first Christmas. Mum and Sam fought over something, and I haven't seen him since.'

Tory kept looking at him, eyes pleading as she continued her story.

Brent's world tumbled around him with her every word.

'I tried to earn money, got a job at McDonald's, but then lost it when Jordie and my other mates came in a few times and disrupted the dining area. They thought it was fun, but management didn't see it that way. I was pretty pissed off with Jordie at the time, but he was entertaining and knew things, so I kept hanging out with him.

'By the time I reached seventeen, I gave up any pretence of going to school. The careers advisor kept encouraging me, telling me I could do whatever I wanted, but with no school certificate, it wasn't true. She arranged a job for me as a receptionist, which, on reflection, was pretty nice of her. Unfortunately, the job didn't last. I got accused of stealing, and they sacked me. I didn't take anything, but Jordie probably did the stealing one day when he picked me up, although he never admitted to anything, and I didn't ask. Jordie owned an old car, his one and only possession. Although it looked like it might fall apart at any time, it was his pride and joy. I remember he told me he stole petrol from time to time to keep it running.

'After the reception job, we did a few break-and-enters into homes to get cash. Then, one day, not long after I turned eighteen, we made a big mistake. We broke into a big house on the hill overlooking the beach.'

CHAPTER 17

Pricilla looked at her watch. It was just before midnight. Intermittent light reflected from the moon as clouds sailed through the dark sky. Jordie parked the car on the roadside outside the mansion's closed wrought-iron gates. Pricilla looked along the curved driveway to an enormous two-storey house.

'They must have lots of shit in there to take,' Jordie said.

'Reckon, jewels and cash for sure,' Pricilla said, rubbing her hands together.

'Yeah, and a big drinks cabinet, with lots of scotch,' Jordie snickered. 'We can have a celebration on them after!'

Dressed in black, the universal uniform of thieves, they exited the car. Jordie pulled a folding ladder from the boot. Behind a tree on the nature strip, hidden from any late-night passing traffic, he leaned the ladder against the fence. They grabbed a backpack each from the boot, and Pricilla softly shut the door.

They hoisted the backpacks over their shoulders, and Pricilla followed Jordie up the ladder and leapt over the fence. To ensure a fast getaway, Pricilla and Jordie awkwardly pulled the ladder through the slats of the fence and set it up on the inside.

Heart racing, Pricilla quietly followed Jordie through the garden. In the shadow of the half-moon, she just made out his crouching body, stepping cautiously between the trees. Clouds masked the moon momentarily, casting an inky darkness across the yard.

Jordie walked around the side of the house to a large window. Beyond the window, Pricilla could see a formal dining room. The window consisted of two sliding panes, and one pane was a few centimetres ajar. Jordie removed a knife from his pocket and slashed the flyscreen. Pricilla tried to slide the window.

'Damn, it's got a window lock. I can't open it any further.'

'No worries. I have the jemmy,' Jordie whispered as he took off his backpack and pulled it from the bag.

'Do you reckon it's alarmed?' Pricilla whispered back.

'Nah, can't see any wiring.'

Jordie jimmied open the window, and they stepped through, into the house. In the darkness, the room looked enormous to Pricilla. The dining room looked the size of her entire house.

On tiptoe, they walked through to the adjoining room. This room was not a formal lounge as Pricilla assumed, but smaller, cosier. By the light of the moon coming through the window, she saw a leather lounge and two tall chairs positioned around a fireplace. Paintings in expensive-looking frames hung on one wall. Lining another wall were bookshelves containing books, trophies, and framed photos. In the half-light, Pricilla assumed they were family photos, but it was too dark to be sure.

'Hey, check this out!' Jordie said as he reached with both hands for an ornate box sitting on the mantle above the fireplace.

The jewelled box had a silver-and-gold frame, set with mother-of-pearl inlay on the sides, and a beautiful mosaic rose set into the lid. In the half-light, Pricilla wondered if the mosaic might be made from rubies or other expensive stones. As Jordie held the jewelled box out to her, she tried to open the lid, but it stayed locked shut. She threw him a questioning look. He shrugged and slid it into his backpack.

Suddenly, shattering the silence, a loud, powerful voice bellowed. The sound came through double doors leading to a stairway. The angry roar sent chills through Pricilla. Terrified, they looked at each other, then towards where the voice had come from. A huge, thickset man, wearing a dressing gown and holding what looked like a gun, stood at the top of the stairs. He began to rush towards them, almost tripping down the stairs.

In unison, they turned and sprinted for the window they had entered through. Pricilla heard the man running toward them. It was still dark; he hadn't turned on the lights. She heard the bang of furniture, a chair tumbling over, and a curse. She hoped that would slow him down.

Once through the window, they dashed towards the fence. The house suddenly lit up, and with light flooding the grounds, the driveway shone bright. They ran through the garden area, away from the lights. Pricilla and Jordie reached the ladder and scrambled up, hurdling over the fence. They left the ladder and threw their backpacks into the car, jumping in after them.

'Go, Jordie, go,' Pricilla yelled.

A sudden loud crack echoed through the night. The dull thud of a bullet hitting metal came a split second later.

'Fuck, go, go, go. He's shooting at us,' Pricilla screamed.

The car fishtailed as it sped off down the street.

Adrenaline coursed through their bodies. Pricilla's heart pounded hard in her chest.

Jordie drove to the next suburb and, with a screech of tyres, pulled over on a side street.

'I've never had someone shoot at me before. Holy shit, what a rush!' Jordie said. His face glowed with the victory of escape.

'Man, was I scared. I thought we were done for,' Pricilla said. She panted, still catching her breath. 'I've never seen anyone so pissed.'

'Yeah, he was mad, alright. We left the damn ladder behind, too. I'll have to nick another one,' Jordie said.

They got out and went around to the back of the car to see where the bullet hit. Jordie pointed to the hole in the boot.

'Fuck, look at that. The bastard put a hole in the side of my car.'

Pricilla looked at Jordie and saw he was beaming. She thought he was secretly pleased with the bullet hole. Something to brag about tomorrow with his mates.

'I reckon the guy with the gun is pretty mean, dangerous even. We should toss the box we nicked. I don't want him finding us if we try to hock it,' Pricilla said.

'Yeah, true that.'

Jordie pulled the box from the backpack and shook it. Nothing rattled.

'It sounds empty.' He walked to a bin sitting on the street for the next day's collection.

'Shame,' he said, looking at the jewelled box. 'But not worth it.'

He opened the bin lid and dropped it in.

* * *

'What happened next was life-changing,' Tory explained.

CHAPTER 18

A week later, a frantic Jordie showed up at her house. She met him at the front door. 'Oh my God, Pricilla, look at this.' He passed her a handwritten note, his hand shaking. 'It was on my car this morning. Stuck under the windscreen wiper.'

As Pricilla read the note, a chill ran along her spine.

You mongrels, you stole my wife's ashes. Return them today or you are dead! I know where you live.

'Fuck! We should have looked in the box. How were we to know it was some bloody old person's ashes?'

Instinctively, Pricilla glanced up and down the street. 'Do you think someone could've followed you?'

'What the fuck does it matter? He said he knows where we live!'

'What if he just knows about you? Where you live? He probably has cameras on the gates at his place and got your number plate. Maybe he doesn't know where I live?'

'Yeah, great. So, it's just me that gets concrete boots. Thanks a lot.'

'Sorry, Jordie. I'm scared. We can't give him back the bloody ashes. They are long gone,' Pricilla said.

'No shit, Sherlock.' Jordie paced up and down on the porch. 'What are we going to do?'

'What if we write him a note to say what we did with the box and drop it at his gate?'

'Fuck no. No way am I going to tell him we chucked his wife in the bin. I'm not going anywhere near his place, or we are corpses for sure.'

'Okay, he might be bluffing, in the hope we will return the box?'

'You had better hope so, Pricilla. Fuck, this is doing my head in!'

* * *

'Jordie told me he wanted to get away, to disappear. He said he'd stay with a mate for a few days. He drove off that afternoon, and I never saw him again,' Tory said.

'The next day, Jordie's mum called me sobbing. She told me Jordie was dead. He'd been killed in a car accident during the night. The police told her his car appeared to have lost control on a bend around the local quarry and gone over the edge. They found his body inside the car.' Tory paused.

'None of his friends lived over that side of the city,' she whispered. 'I knew it wasn't an accident.'

* * *

Pricilla hung up the call and ran the four blocks to Jordie's house. No one answered her knocks. She'd assumed Jordie's mum had called her from home. Pricilla sat on their back verandah and cried.

She felt alone and afraid. Jordie was the one person she had relied on, the one person she could trust. Now he was gone. Could she have saved him? What if they had gone away together? Would she be dead too?

The funeral broke her heart. Pricilla stood at the cemetery next to a few of his other mates. She saw his mum, with tears streaming down her face. She seemed to fold in grief, someone helping her to sit on the chairs placed beside the grave for the family. There wasn't a wake, at least not one Jordie's mates got invited to. After the funeral, she walked around for hours, grieving and lost, wondering what she would do now without her best friend. As darkness set in, she headed towards home.

Pricilla turned off the footpath to her house, and as she looked up, she saw the front door partially open, hanging oddly. She slipped sideways through the door. Her mum sat on the lounge with the television blaring, a cigarette hanging from her lips.

'What have you been up to, you stupid cow? You've made a real enemy now. The bastard kicked in the door,' her mum hissed. 'He called 'ere looking for you, and someth'n you stole. I don't wan' shit happening 'ere. This is the last straw, you lazy, useless bitch. You can piss off now. I don' want you ever back 'ere again.'

Pricilla looked at her mum in horror. The guy knew her address and had come after her. She understood her mum meant every word. Where would she hide? Where would she stay? Pricilla rushed to her room and pushed the dresser back from the wall. She pulled out the clothes and her few possessions, tossed everything into a sports bag, then snuck out the back door to unearth the money hidden in the yard. She slipped the money into her pocket and walked back through the house, past her mother still slouched on the couch, and out through the wonky front door without looking back. Neither said goodbye.

* * *

'And that was the last time I set eyes on my mother,' Tory said. 'The money got me by for a while. I hid at my friend Glenda's house for a few weeks. I changed my name. Luckily, I didn't have a criminal record, so could apply online. I used Glenda's address, and in a few weeks got a new ID in the post. With my new identity, I took a bus to Sydney. I couch surfed until I got a job and rented a room. I did the course at TAFE. It was such a wake-up call. I lived honestly. I worked hard, saved money, and after a few years, moved here and met you.'

Brent leaned back, studying her.

'Do you know his name, the guy who wanted to kill you and Jordie?'

'Yes, we were really stupid.' Tory hung her head. 'I found out his name is Anton Solo. I read in the paper he was a kingpin of the tobacco trade when Australia grew the stuff. He is very rich.'

'You told me your mum's dead. Is she?'

'Oh, Brent, I don't know. I haven't been back or in contact with anyone since I left. I didn't tell Glenda about my new name, so no one can get in contact with me. Mum's horrible, a disgrace. I don't want to speak or connect with her ever again.'

'Tory, I feel like I hardly know you now.'

Tory started to cry again, broken-hearted. 'Oh, Brent, I am so sorry. By the time I met you, it had been three years with the new name, and my life looked good. I assumed I'd outrun my past. I couldn't tell you in case you didn't want to see me again. Then, when you asked me to marry you, it seemed too late. There was never a good time.'

* * *

'I just can't comprehend what you have done, what you kept from me.' Brent said, shaking his head. His beautiful wife, lying to him all this time. His mind kept coming back to Tory having a past she didn't share with him. He felt betrayed; his stomach churned. He turned to Tory.

'I'm going to Mum and Dad's. I need to talk to them.' He started the truck and angrily slammed it into gear. Did he even believe this fantastical story Tory told? Who was this person sitting next to him, the one he loved, or thought he loved? Maybe his father could guide him, provide some clarity.

CHAPTER 19

Gordon and Gail heard Brent's truck screech to a halt outside their home. They rushed to the front door and met Brent as he walked into the house. They knew instantly, by his troubled look, and Tory's distraught face as she followed him, something was seriously wrong. Gail glanced sideways at Gordon.

'Something's happened,' she said, her eyebrows furrowed with concern.

Gail hurried Brent and Tory through the door and into the lounge.

'Son, what is it? What's wrong?' Gordon asked, alarmed.

Brent stood and choked out Tory's story, his confusion clear as he stumbled over his words. As Brent ranted, he watched Tory first pace up and down, then sit on an arm of the lounge. One moment, his voice rose in anger, fuming; the next, he whispered in despair at the lies. Gordon was empathetic and calming. Gail was neither of those things. Her face coloured, and she swivelled around to confront Tory.

The visceral response from his mother stunned Brent. Gail launched into a scathing attack on Tory.

Gail became ferocious, questioning Tory's past as well as her commitment to Brent and her granddaughter. Brent listened, stunned at his mother's wrath, as she became the protective lioness, her voice rising with every spoken word. She attacked the dishonesty and danger Tory had risked on her son and granddaughter.

'How dare you keep this from your husband, from us?' Gail challenged Tory. 'We have done nothing but support you, and now we see you are not the person you pretend to be.' Gail's forehead creased, her jaw tensed, lips thinned.

Brent noticed his mother's hand was shaking with anger.

'How can you be so duplicitous?' Gail spat.

'Careful,' Gordon said, laying a calming hand on Gail's arm as Tory stormed outside to the garden. 'Don't say what can't be undone.'

* * *

Tory's legs dangled as she sat in the hanging chair on the verandah. The chair faced the beautifully landscaped suburban backyard. The yard was larger than most in the street. Her in-laws loved gardening and spent hours creating the serene space she now looked over. Birds chirped loudly as a gentle warmth from the sun on the patio radiated through Tory.

Tory barely noticed its beauty or the warmth as she tried to calm herself after storming out of the house. She took a deep breath.

That bloody mother-in-law should mind her own business. Who died and made her queen? The words screamed inside Tory's head.

Infuriatingly, Brent didn't jump in to support Tory. Instead, he stood there saying nothing as Gail ranted on about Tory's past and commitment to the family. Gordon stood silently next to Brent too, not contradicting Gail.

'Bloody gutless wonders,' Tory mused under her breath.

Damn police check!

Tory knew she was in trouble. Her marriage was on the line. Brent might never trust her again. Tory felt at a loss to know what she would do if Brent started hating her. What would happen with Laura? Would Brent take their daughter off her? Overwhelmed, tears slid down her face as she waited for Brent to take her home.

Finally, Brent walked out of the house towards her. He barely looked at her.

'Come on. We have to pick up Laura,' he said as he walked past her.

Tory wiped her eyes and stood. Afraid to speak, head down, she followed Brent to the truck. On the way to the childcare centre, silence filled the cabin. It was a small relief for Tory to hear Laura's bubbly voice on the way home.

As soon as they went inside the house, Laura ran straight to her room to change out of her school uniform.

'Brent,' Tory said, trembling as she looked into his eyes. 'My life is in your hands. You and Laura mean everything to me. I am sorry I didn't tell you about my past. I've never deliberately done anything to hurt you. I love you. You and Laura are my life. Please forgive me,' she pleaded.

Brent looked at her, his face showing the anger and hurt he felt. Unable to speak, he shrugged, turned, and walked from the room as Tory sobbed quietly, completely bereft. What would happen to her now?

CHAPTER 20

Tory lay awake in bed staring at the dark ceiling, her mind conjuring worst-case scenarios. She heard every creak the house made. She imagined how devastated she would be if Brent could not forgive her and asked for a divorce. Tory felt so alone now. Her hand reached out to Brent's side of the bed. The empty, cold sheets compounded her misery, and she let out an involuntary sob.

Brent didn't come into their room that evening. Instead, he slept in the lounge room, on the couch. After they put Laura in bed, silence filled the house. Brent didn't speak or even look at her. It was unbearable. She sat in the silence until it drove her crazy. Finally, she went to bed, hoping Brent might follow her. She loved Brent with all her heart. He was her metronome in life; she lived and breathed to the rhythm of his very being. It made her content, and now her life, her happiness, their marriage … It was all in peril.

I am such a fool. Why didn't I tell him?

Tory understood why, though. If he found out what sort of person she was in her youth, if he realised all the stupid and illegal things she had done, he wouldn't want to be with her. No one trusted a thief. She was scum. She'd spent her adult life running from her past, hiding from the terrible things she'd done. After a few years with Brent, Tory started to believe the new person she'd become, to believe she deserved a middle-class life. She'd stopped thinking of her past and convinced herself she'd become someone else. Until today.

'*People get what they deserve. You can't outrun your past. Something always catches up with you,*' Tory remembered her mother snarling at her one day.

At the time, Tory thought her mother was just being a bitch, but now, she reckoned, her mum had been right on the money. What a fool she'd been to think she deserved a middle-class life. She didn't deserve Brent, their house, her beautiful daughter. Gail saw it, Tory understood. Gail could tell she wasn't worthy of her son, which explained why she had been so horrified when Tory fell pregnant and Brent married her. *Something he probably regrets now*, she thought.

Her mother was right. She couldn't outrun her past. The time had arrived for her to face up to her past behaviour. Brent would be her judge. He would decide if she could atone for her actions. Her happiness, her future, hung by a thread, and it made her ill. Her chest ached, and her head pounded. Tory could not remember feeling more miserable than she did right now.

Unable to bear it anymore, Tory pushed back the doona and tiptoed to the lounge room. She stood in the doorway and watched Brent sleep. His head faced toward the back of the couch and awkwardly rested on his arm. He didn't look comfortable.

Brent spoke in the darkness, making Tory jump.

'Were you really in fear of this man, or was that just teenager fantasy?' Brent asked, his voice quiet.

Tory sat on the floor, leaning back against the couch, relieved Brent was speaking to her.

'He scared me, Brent. I know he killed Jordie or had him killed. I would've been next. I'm sure of it.'

'Do you know anything about him? Who he is?'

'I looked him up after I got to Sydney,' Tory said. 'He ran a big syndicate growing tobacco back when it was legal. The government gave them all big payout compensations when they banned tobacco farming. But from what I can gather, he was already wealthy. He had two boys. One of his sons got killed in an accident, and the other one is in jail. Anton has never been found guilty of any criminal activity, as far as I can tell.'

'So why did he have a gun?'

'Yeah, right. I am sure he's involved in crime, just never caught, or he's been able to bribe himself out of trouble. People seemed afraid of writing about him. I remember seeing one story describing a cluster of unexplained deaths linked to the tobacco trade. The article insinuated a few of the older tobacco families, including Anton's, may have been involved, but no one got arrested. There was only one brief article reporting on the son going to jail. He probably threatened journos.'

'He must be pretty old now,' Brent said.

'Yes. He'd be in his eighties, I think. A year after I went to Sydney, I saw a newspaper article reporting on a speedboat accident. Two people died when their boat exploded in flames. His youngest son drove and died in the boat.'

'That must hurt. Dead wife, dead son, other son in jail.'

'Yep, and we threw the wife's ashes into the tip. How he must hate me.' Tory shuddered.

Brent's arm reached over Tory's shoulders, pulling her into a close hug.

'Let's go to bed. We can talk more about this tomorrow,' Brent said as he stood from the couch, holding his hand out for Tory to clasp, and pulled her up from the floor. They slowly walked hand-in-hand to the bedroom.

CHAPTER 21

Anton Solo pulled the buzzing mobile phone from his pocket, looked at the caller display showing an unknown number, and answered with a gruff, 'Yeah.'

'Do you still want to know about that woman?' a male voice spoke.

Anton sat up straighter in his chair, his attention sharpened. His fingers habitually brushed over his head, which in recent years had become devoid of hair.

He'd been waiting for this call for seven years. He'd tried to remain hopeful but feared the call would never come. At age eighty-two, his time was running out. Only recently, he'd begun to imagine reasons the call hadn't come, musing wistfully that perhaps she was dead.

'Oh, very much indeed,' Anton responded, his heart racing.

He knew one day she'd make a mistake. She would do something to come to the attention of the police, and his friend would be alerted and call him.

The night the two intruders breached the security of his home, and overturned his life, remained vivid in his mind.

* * *

Anton woke to the sound of soft footsteps and whispers in a downstairs room. Ears pricked, listening carefully, he eased himself out of his king-sized bed, a bed he nowadays only shared with the finer escort women. He wrapped his dressing gown around his naked body and silently walked into the wardrobe. Reaching behind a shelf of hats and golf clothing, his fingers wrapped around the smooth steel of the hidden pistol, sliding it from its place. From a nearby drawer, he extracted a loaded magazine and quietly and efficiently slid it into the weapon.

Barefoot, stepping slowly, Anton reached the top of the stairway leading to the dining and sitting rooms. He could see two young people below, a boy and a girl. Both wore dark clothing. The short purple hair of the girl, visible with the moonlight shining through the window, stood out. He saw a window open, and the flyscreen, sliced in half, flapping slightly in the breeze.

Anger surged through Anton.

'Who the fuck are you?' he yelled as his large body raced down the stairs, his arm raising the pistol as he ran. Two horrified faces looked up at him. The figures quickly pivoted and sprinted towards the window.

He chased after them. At the bottom of the stairs, he ran to the dining room.

'Oof,' Anton grunted as he collided with a chair. The pair leapt out the window and sprinted into the garden. He ran to the next room, the kitchen, and opened the back door. He flicked a switch for the lights in the yard as he stepped out.

He saw them climb over a ladder and dive into a car. He lifted the pistol, took aim, and fired. A spark bounced off the car as the bullet hit the boot, and he stood watching as the car flew along the street, taillights disappearing around the corner.

'Those scumbag shits. I hope they have nightmares for months,' he muttered as he walked back inside.

Better shut the window, Anton thought.

He turned on the dining room lights and walked to the window. Something caught his eye. An empty place on the mantelpiece, usually occupied by his most treasured possession, taunted him. His guts constricted as if someone had punched him.

'Noooooo!' He bent, doubled over, roaring.

The ashes of his beautiful wife, Sophia, no longer sat in their pride of place. Anton, desperate, looked around the downstairs rooms, hoping to find the precious box dropped on the floor by the thieves as they fled. Nothing. He grabbed a torch from the kitchen cupboard and stepped into the yard. Frantic, he followed the path the two had taken as they fled his home, his torch searching from side to side as he walked to the fence. The moon threw up shadows from the trees and bushes in the garden, and he searched amongst the leaves and branches. He walked up and back to check, again and again, desperate. Unable to find the precious jewelled box containing Sophia's ashes, Anton looked for hours, hoping beyond hope the two had dropped their loot as they ran. He checked inside again. Nothing. Reluctantly, he faced reality. He knew they didn't drop it. The little bastards stole the box, his most precious box.

'I'll kill those bastards,' Anton swore.

Sophia meant everything to Anton. They met and married young. Anton had gone to a neighbour's party in his hometown of

Myrtleford. He spotted Sophia, who was visiting from Melbourne, and did not take his eyes off her for the rest of the evening. Anton worked on his parents' tobacco farm, a farm he later inherited. That night, Sophia agreed to come back to visit him, and three months later, they got married. In Anton's eyes, Sophia was beautiful and could do no wrong. He treated her like a princess. She didn't ask for much, but Anton gave her everything.

Sadly, Sophia contracted an infection after having their second son, resulting in her being unable to have any further children. When she confessed she felt a failure, Anton was dismayed at her misery. As a gift, he built her a luxurious home in which she could raise their two precious sons. With pride, they nurtured their children as they grew into adults.

Their family was popular in the tobacco-growing community. Anton's farm was successful, becoming one of the most lucrative in Australia. He expanded, buying more properties in the region. Their wealth grew, but that was not enough to save Sophia after her diagnosis of breast cancer. To Anton's horror, Sophia died less than a year after her diagnosis. It ripped his heart out.

At her bedside, despite her gentle disagreement, he promised her there would be no one else. She would always be closest to his heart. After her death, to house her ashes, Anton commissioned a reproduction Fabergé casket box, with mother-of-pearl inlay and gilded filigree, inset with precious stones. As always, only the best for his beautiful wife. The box, a work of art with precious contents, always remained in pride of place in his homes. The tiny key used to lock the box, he carried inside the large snuff ring he wore on his right hand. Nothing could bring Sophia back, he knew. However, talking to the beautiful box in the lonely evenings somehow brought Sophia closer.

Eyeballing the empty space on the mantle, Anton's rage mounted. The pressure in his head thumped and beads of sweat glistened on his forehead as he clenched his fists and pounded his thighs.

'Fuck, fuck, fuck!' he bellowed.

Anton stormed to his home office, flicked on the light, hit his keyboard, and logged onto the security system. He saw the faces of both intruders on the dining room footage.

'You are both dead!' he raged, his finger pointing to the screen.

Anton switched to the security footage of the front gate and fence line. After a few minutes of scrolling through the timeline, he identified the car the two used. Zooming in, Anton read the number plate.

'Got you,' he exhaled, sitting back in his chair.

Anton pulled the mobile phone from the pocket of his dressing gown and dialled a friend. Well, not so much a friend, but the son of a good friend he once helped with a deposit on his home. He was owed. Anton strategically gifted the young man his house deposit, no strings, just a favour. The man worked at the court-house, with access to the police database and other useful intel. Anton anticipated, rightly so, it seemed, that this man would come in handy at some point in time.

'Hello,' a sleepy voice said.

'Graham, this is Anton Solo. I need you to check something for me.'

'Mr Solo, it's three in the morning. What has happened? How can I help?' The voice was suddenly alert.

'I need you to look up a number plate. Find out who owns it and their address.'

'No worries. I can do that first thing when I get into the office. I can't do it now, or it will raise suspicion. I hope that's okay, Mr Solo?'

'Fine. Just get back to me as soon as you can.' Anton recited the number plate to Graham and ended the call.

Anton's relationship-building paid off. Graham called at ten o'clock the following morning. He had a name, Jorden Watts. He had an address.

CHAPTER 22

Anger roared through Anton as the scum told him they threw his precious Sophia's ashes into a bin. His beautiful wife disrespected in death, her ashes gone with the city trash to the tip.

Earlier, at a convenience store, the young man stopped to buy smokes. He didn't see Anton's men tailing him in their dark car. They were waiting, standing against Jordie's vehicle, as he walked out of the store.

Jordie looked up and noticed the men.

'Hey, what're do'in?'

The men stepped forward without saying a word, discreetly and firmly manhandling Jordie into the back seat of his car. One guy roughly sat beside him.

'Hey, get your hands offa me. Let me go.' Jodie's protest earned him a solid punch to the guts.

'Asshole, hand me your fuckin' keys.'

Ashen-faced, holding his stomach and panting, trying to regain his breath, Jordie fumbled as he pulled the keys from his pocket. The mountain of a man sitting in the driver's seat stretched out a gloved hand, and Jordie dropped the keys into his palm. They drove off. Jordie stared out the window as they drove past the main drag and headed to the outskirts of town.

'Whe're you taking me? What do ya want?' Jordie trembled.

Neither man said a word.

'What the hell, man? Where're we going?'

In silence, they kept driving.

Jordie had a bad feeling tonight would not end well. His guts hurt, and the big guy next to him looked like he could crush Jordie with his bare hands. All he could do was look out the window as the homes flashed by, then thinned, as they headed away from the city centre. Finally, the car slowed and pulled over in a dark street atop a hill, where Anton waited. The town lights twinkled in the distance.

The men roughly dragged Jordie from the car and stood him in front of Anton, who was holding a golf club he'd pulled from the set in the boot of his Mercedes. Jordie's knees turned to jelly in fear as he recognised the man.

Anton held the club high over Jordie's head.

'You little punk. Think you and your girlfriend can break into my home and steal. Where the fuck is the box you took?'

Rage tore through Anton. He brought the raised club down hard. The young man fell and cowered on the ground as he was hit again and again. Jordie trembled, cowering before Anton as he begged for his life.

'Mister. I'm sorry. We chucked it in a bin across town from your joint. I can't remember what street it was. We panicked. You scared the living shit outa us when you fired that shot.'

Rage overpowered Anton. He didn't wait to get the name of the girl accomplice. He viciously brought the club down and hit the boy, again and again.

It was his two trusted assassins who pulled him off the battered and bleeding Jordie.

'Enough now, Anton,' one said. He firmly put his hand on Anton's arm, holding the club, stopping him from bringing it down again. 'Hit him more, and we won't be able to make it look like an accident.'

Anton nodded, lowered the club, and reluctantly stepped backwards. His shoulders heaved from exertion.

Death is too good for this scum, Anton thought as he panted, trying to catch his breath.

Anton watched his men roughly pick up Jordie and bungle him into the driver's seat. They put the car in gear, weighed the accelerator down with a heavy rock, and sent it catapulting over the side of the hill. Without speaking, they stood watching the car roll down the embankment, flipping over and over, until it stopped, propped at an angle on rocks twenty metres below them. Jordie's head, shoulders, and one arm stuck out from the side window, hanging lifeless.

'Right, let's find that little bitch sidekick and fix her up too,' Anton demanded. He turned and briskly walked to his car before throwing the golf club into the boot and sitting in the back seat. His men chauffeured him home.

* * *

Out of respect for the mother and not wanting to implicate himself in the death of her son, Anton waited several days, until the morning of the funeral, before calling at Jordie's home with flowers.

'My condolences, Mrs Watts. I am sorry for your loss,' Anton said. He handed the flowers to the bereaved woman standing in the doorway.

'I don't think we have met. Did you know Jorden?' she asked.

'A little,' Anton lied. 'I met Jorden and his girlfriend at a football game. I wanted to offer my condolences to her as well, but I don't have her name.'

'Oh, that would be Pricilla Banes,' Mrs Watts said, then told him her address.

Anton smiled to himself as he walked out the gate. That was too easy.

* * *

Just as he was losing hope, his contact came through. Graham's call reinvigorated Anton. At long last, he was going to avenge his wife. To get payback for the debt owed. He was going to enjoy calling it in.

Anton listened as Graham explained how a recent fingerprint search by police had revealed the new name Pricilla used. A query set up in the system years before had pinged him with an alert only hours ago. She now went by the name of Tory Packenham. She lived in Aloma at the same address as a man with the same surname, assumedly her husband. Anton was familiar with Aloma. It was a city not far from where he grew up. He travelled there on the odd occasion when he was young, on school trips, and then later, shopping with his wife. He hadn't frequented Aloma regularly, however, so wouldn't be recognised there. He was confident of that.

Anton hung up from the call, smirking. His moment of revenge had arrived. As keen as he was to finish this, he knew he needed to take things slowly. Not make any mistakes. Seven years ago, he could count on at least one of his sons to help him. Back then, he also retained a number of security men who supported activities, such as what played out with Jorden. Now, nearly a decade later, with one son dead, the other in jail, and no security staff on payroll, he would have to either recruit or do the deed himself.

Anton wanted revenge. He could taste it. He decided this was a job he'd enjoy doing himself. *That cheap whore of a woman. Lowlife scum with no respect*, Anton fumed. *She will end up dead like her boyfriend.*

Anton booked a midway motel, packed a bag, putting the Glock in first, and then tossed it into the boot of his car. He didn't have a plan for doing the deed just yet but was in a hurry to lay eyes on the bitch. He would figure it out when he got there. He did hope he would get to see the fear in her eyes as he pulled the trigger, though.

Putting the car into gear, he set off for the ten-hour drive.

CHAPTER 23

Brent left for work early. He'd been moody and silent all morning, eyes avoiding Tory as he got dressed and then walked out the door without eating breakfast. Last night, after Brent's conciliatory words, she felt a small glimmer of hope that he might forgive her. However, his silence this morning sent her right back to despair. Nan's car meant Tory could resume the normal early drop-off to school. Tory noticed Laura sensed the tension, too, as she threw her schoolbag over her shoulder and gave Tory a hug before getting into the car.

Nan's car brought freedom for Tory. She couldn't believe how hamstrung she'd been without a car, completely dependent on others. After doing the school drop, a relieved Tory arrived at work on time and without hassle.

She worked contentedly all morning, preferring to focus on work rather than her train wreck of a marriage. At morning tea, she even gave cheek to some of the crew.

'Hey, Tory, that was a bit quick for you,' Glen quipped. 'Driving that antique orange mobile make you invincible?'

Tory laughed along with the others in the office.

'Piss off, Glen. It's a glamour mobile,' she said, still chuckling.

Tory picked up her mobile as it rang.

'Tory, it's Jane from school. Laura's in sickbay with a headache. She needs to be picked up.'

'Oh no, is she alright?'

'Yes, just complaining of a headache and a bit teary.'

'Okay, thanks for calling me. I'll be there as soon as I can.'

Tory stood and walked to Frank's office.

'Sorry, Frank, but the school has just called. Laura is sick, and I need to take her home.'

The look on Frank's face startled Tory. It was not a sympathetic one. He frowned, and her heart sank.

'Tory, I don't know how much time I can keep giving you. While Laura has to be picked up, you've spent an awful lot of time off work lately. Is there someone else who can do it?'

'Oh,' Tory said. She was momentarily stumped. While Frank's reaction upset her, she tried not to let it show. It never crossed Tory's mind that Frank would not want her to pick up Laura. With Brent away on a job, the only option available to her was to call Gail. Reluctantly, she nodded to Frank.

'I'll call my mother-in-law and see if she can help out,' Tory said. She walked back to her desk and pulled out her phone. It would take all Tory had to call Gail. The Gail who currently hated her. The Gail who only yesterday abused her for her past and her secrets. First, Tory dialled Brent, hoping beyond hope he would pick up so she could ask him to call his mother. After a minute of the ringtone, Tory knew there was no choice but to suck it up. Given any other option, Tory would not be making this phone call. She listened to the phone ring, and then Gail answered.

'Hello.'

'Gail, it's Tory.'

'What can I do for you?' Gail said. Tory heard the curtness in her voice.

'Laura is sick, and I can't get time off work. Can you pick her up?'

'Of course I can do that, Tory. I'm always happy to help with Laura when things get too much for you. I can get her in half an hour.'

Bristling at Gail's words, Tory kept her voice pleasant. She needed Gail now and felt trapped into playing nice.

'Thanks, Gail. You have the key. Take her home, and I will get there as soon as I can get away from work.' Tory hung up. As usual, Gail left her feeling inadequate and angry.

It seemed like only yesterday Brent and Tory walked Laura to her first day of school. Laura looked so grown-up in her school uniform. The backpack she carried seemed so big, at least half her size. As they approached the school gates, they watched the children milling around, some in tears, others excited to see friends. Parents hugged teary children. Some parents were teary themselves. On the quadrangle at the front of the main office building, a game of handball played out.

As they approached the gate, an excited and confident Laura shrieked as she saw her friends, waving frantically as she ran towards them. She turned her head, without slowing, to call 'see ya' to Tory and Brent.

'Well, what an anticlimax,' Brent said. He looked at Tory, who nodded, tears welling in her eyes. 'Let's get a coffee and ponder how Miss Precocious will go.'

Tory forced her thoughts back to the present. She hoped Laura wasn't too sick. She would have preferred to pick her up and watch over her. She spent the rest of the day distracted, worrying about Laura, Gail's undermining, and Frank's response to her request for time off. Frank's reaction was in stark contrast to his usual respect for her. It concerned her that things were heading in a dark direction at work.

* * *

The next evening, dressed in her best blue-and-white blouse, darker-blue soft-pleated pants, and silver heels, Tory looked into her bedroom mirror. Her short blonde hair stood obediently spiked, and she thought she looked good as she turned sideways, checking out her back view. Tory puckered her lips and applied the finishing touch of lipstick. She was meeting Carolyn for a night out on the town. While partying was probably the last thing she should be doing at the moment, the drinks organised last week offered a good chance for the two of them to catch up away from work and home, and she was looking forward to it.

Unfortunately, Brent's training night coincided with their plans, so last week, Brent asked Gail to mind Laura. It was a shame, Tory thought, with Laura being sick yesterday, that they needed to call on Gail two days in a row. At least Laura was feeling better today, and it had been Brent who asked Gail, not her.

Tory's phone pinged.

'That's Caro. She's out the front. Thanks again, Gail, for watching Laura,' Tory said. She bent and kissed Laura, who was sitting and drawing at the kitchen table. 'You be good for Grandma.'

'I will, I promise. See you tomorrow, Mummy.'

Tory let out a sigh of relief as she sat next to Carolyn in the back seat of the taxi. Carolyn looked stunning as usual, dressed in a hot-pink pantsuit with pink platform heels. Her hair tied high in a ponytail made her look glamorous, and she wore a large diamanté ring and bracelet.

'You look gorgeous.'

'Thanks. You too, girlfriend.'

'I'm really looking forward to this, after the few weeks I've had!'

'Me too. You've had a pretty rough time, that's for sure.'

'You don't know the half of it. I will fill you in when I get my first drink,' Tory said, thinking of how she might reveal to Carolyn her previous identity. She was nervous and worried about her friend's reaction. In fact, if she thought about it, Tory was terrified. What if she didn't like what she heard or became offended with Tory for not sharing her secret earlier? Tory knew she needed to tell her. Carolyn visited her and Brent too often. She'd sense something going on. It was clear she had no option but to tell Caro her story. Butterflies filled her stomach.

The taxi dropped them at a busy bar on the main street. Carolyn linked arms with Tory, and they walked through the doors together. They were greeted by a noisy bar full of people with drinks in hand, standing around or sitting on stools at tall tables made from reclaimed wood. Fake ivy hung down the redbrick walls, suspended from large wooden beams that lined the ceiling. Dimmed lights provided a lost-in-the-woods ambience. Background music played. The place was jumping.

They sat at the one free table towards the back of the room.

Tory wove her way back through the crowd to the bar and ordered them a cocktail each. Holding the drinks high in front of her so as not to be bumped, Tory returned to the table. She placed a Margarita in front of Carolyn. The Cosmopolitan was hers. Sitting side by side, facing toward the centre of the room, they watched the comings and goings at the bar as they talked.

'So,' started Tory, 'tell me how things are going with Karl.'

'He is so nice,' Carolyn said. Her eyes went dreamy. 'He is the perfect man, six feet tall, dark and handsome. Muscles everywhere, but not too big. And he likes me. Perfect really. So I am playing hard to get.'

'What?' Tory spluttered on her drink. 'Why would you do that?'

'I am sick of men, boys, just wanting me for a fling. If Karl wants me to sleep with him, he needs to be in for the long haul. I want a ring, kids, the full shebang. Maybe not on the first date,' Carolyn added with a laugh, 'but eventually.'

'You stick to that!' Tory said, grinning. 'I hope it works out. He is a nice man. I like how he is always smiling when he comes to the office.'

'Me too,' Carolyn said.

The moment had come for Tory. It was now or never. She sipped her cocktail, and taking a deep breath, she looked toward Carolyn and spoke.

'Okay, I am in a bit of strife with Brent. I need to tell you something. You can't tell anyone else, including Karl. The only people who know are Brent, his parents, and the police.'

Carolyn's eyes filled with concern.

'What is it, girlfriend?'

'Before I met you, when I left home, I had a different name. I made an enemy and needed to get away from him. I changed my name and moved to Sydney.' Tory told her friend the full story, leaving nothing out.

'So, with the theft, then the fingerprints we did, my other name showed up on the police check. I hadn't told Brent about that part of my past. He's livid.'

'Shit. Bombshell, girlfriend. I am sure he will calm down. He loves you, Tory.'

'I hope so. I have never seen him so upset. His mum went spare when she found out, too. She hates me,' said Tory. She miserably gulped down her drink. Too fast for a cocktail. She would regret it tomorrow.

Carolyn looked at her with intent, her face serious, then she smiled.

'Okay, while I process a whole other you, let's have another drink and then a dance,' Carolyn said. She stood to go to the bar.

'You aren't mad at me?'

'Why would I be?' Carolyn looked down at Tory.

'Because I didn't tell you earlier. I've kept this big secret from you.'

'If you didn't tell Brent, why would I expect you to tell me? You had your reasons for not telling us. You didn't want to risk your safety. Why tell someone you'd only just met? You didn't know who to trust.' She bent down and gave Tory a reassuring kiss on the cheek before turning towards the bar.

Filled with relief, Tory watched her make her way to the bar. She hadn't known what to expect, but Caro's reaction came as a welcome surprise. What a good friend she was. Tory watched as Carolyn was stopped two separate times by men flirting with her and likely offering to buy her a drink. *Carolyn is so attractive. Men just gravitate to her*, Tory thought. *Karl will be lucky if he can catch her.*

Carolyn returned carrying two cocktails and sat down.

'Stop looking so sad. Brent loves you. It will be alright. He just needs time to process things. You are his family, like you are mine. We love you. It will be alright. I promise.'

'Thanks, Caro,' Tory said. She put her hand over Carolyn's. 'You are my family, and I love you too.'

Tory and Carolyn meant so much to each other. Except for Nan, Carolyn's family lived in New Zealand and weren't in regular contact. Tory and Carolyn provided stability and sisterly care for each other.

'Who else could I rely on to come out with me for crazy nights and dancing, and to fend off the male species?' Tory laughed.

'Too right, girlfriend,' said Carolyn. She lifted her cocktail, touched Tory's with a ding, and took a sip.

CHAPTER 24

The next day, Tory woke with a pounding head.

That one more was one too many, she thought as she sat at her desk.

The two headache pills she swallowed with her breakfast coffee were still to kick in. Carolyn walked in a short time later, looking how Tory felt. Tory nodded to Carolyn, who groaned in response as she walked past.

After her lunch break, when Tory forced herself to consume a can of Coke and a tomato-and-cheese toasted sandwich, her phone rang with an internal call.

'Tory, there are some men at the front desk asking to see you,' the receptionist told her.

Tory walked to the showroom and looked around. Two men, one with a large bodybuilder frame and the other tall and thin, stood waiting for her. She didn't recognise either of them.

'Tory Packenham?' the thin one asked.

'Yes, can I help you?'

'You can pay your debts,' he said, passing her a letter.

Tory read the letter and paled.

'You owe Johnston Holdings four and a half thousand dollars. We're here to collect payment.'

The men stepped forward, into Tory's personal space. She instinctively stepped backwards and raised her hands as if to hold them off.

'I'm sorry. I didn't incur this debt. It's a mistake. There's been fraudulent use of my details to gain credit. The police are aware and investigating. I'll give this letter to them to sort out,' Tory said, waving the letter toward the men.

'No good. We need payment now,' the bodybuilder said as he puffed himself up, standing taller, towering over Tory. She glanced around, frightened, just as Frank walked into the showroom.

'Is everything alright? Can I help you, gentlemen?'

'Everything is fine. We're just leaving,' the thin man said. 'Tory, we'll talk to you again.' Both gave her a menacing look as they turned and walked out.

Frank looked at Tory and paused before speaking.

'Tory, I think you need to take some time off work. You need to sort out your debt situation. We can't have debt collectors chasing you here. You can use your annual leave, and after that, take leave without pay for a while, until it's sorted.'

Tory's heart dropped.

'I'm sorry, Frank. I'll speak to the police again. I don't understand why the men came here to talk to me. They shouldn't do that.'

Tory only had four days of annual leave accrued. She used her leave to cover the recent Christmas break and time off with Laura before she started school. Forced leave would mean she wouldn't get paid. They'd need to live off Brent's income.

Tory returned to her desk, logged out of the computer, picked up her handbag, and left the building. Carolyn was not at her desk. She'd tell her later about this disaster.

When Brent arrived home after work, Tory told him about the debt collectors and being sent home from work. He threw his hands in the air.

'Shit, Tory, I don't make that much money that we can do without your salary. You've got to talk to Frank to see if you can get your job back. Maybe go in Monday, after he has calmed down?'

'Thanks for your concern, Brent. Two blokes come to work to intimidate me. Which they did quite well, thank you, and you don't even mention that!' Tory yelled.

'That's a different issue, Tory. Of course, that worries me, but we need your salary.'

Tory looked at Brent. Her mouth quivered, and she burst into tears. Everything was going wrong.

At that moment, Laura, wearing her pyjamas, walked into the room, her face creased with concern.

'Are you and Daddy getting divorced? Sara's parents are divorced. She spends every second weekend at her dad's. He buys her ice cream and lets her watch YouTube until nine o'clock.'

'No, darling. We are not getting a divorce.' Tory looked at Brent quickly and then back to Laura. At least, she hoped they wouldn't be.

'We are having a little fight. I am sorry we were so loud and worried you.'

'Okay, but if you do, can I watch YouTube too?'

'It's not happening, bub. Time for bed,' Brent said. He picked Laura up and carried her to her bedroom.

Tory watched them go as she wiped the tears from her face. She needed a plan. She needed to work out how to move forward. To get rid of the fraud and get her job back. At the same time, she needed Brent to forgive her for not telling him about her past.

CHAPTER 25

Since she didn't have to go to work, Tory took the opportunity to spend some one-on-one time with Laura and walk her to school. She wanted to reassure Laura that her parents loved each other and everything was fine. Tory felt an urgent need to protect Laura from fear and uncertainty. Tory held her hand and led her across the road to the footpath. The morning sun warmed them, the heat promised for later in the day yet to arrive.

Laura complained most of the way.

'Why do we have to walk, Mummy? Can't you drive Nan's car?'

'Walking is good for you. The day is nice. I thought the walk might do us both good, and we can chat.'

Laura looked at her as if she had two heads. 'There's nothing I want to *chat* about. If we drove, I'd get to school early to play with Erin.'

'Well, too bad. We are walking now,' Tory said.

Laura pouted and sulked. They walked in silence. As soon as they arrived at the school gate, Laura slipped her hand from Tory's and ran off towards her friends.

Well, that went well.

As she returned home, her mobile buzzed.

'Hello, Tory. Detective Blunt here.' Her voice sounded curt.

'Hello, Detective.'

After the scare at work yesterday, Tory emailed the detective a copy of the demand notice and an explanation of the intimidation attempt. Tory hadn't spoken to the detectives since the meeting about her alias, and she was unsure what sort of reception her email would receive, or even if the detectives were still working on her case.

'I received your message yesterday.'

'Detective, I'm sorry about our last meeting and my other name. I should've told you.'

'Look, Tory, it would have been better if you did tell us. It put a real dint in my trust for you. But I understand why you didn't. It doesn't change how we are investigating your case.'

'That's a relief. Thank you. I appreciate your professionalism, and I hope I can restore your trust somehow.'

'No omissions of facts and complete and truthful statements from hereon will be the best way.'

Chastened, Tory changed the subject.

'Is there anything you can do about the debt notice and collection guys?'

'I've contacted the company and discussed the debt and the behaviour of their debt collectors. They agreed to put the demand for money on hold until we can confirm how the goods were to be paid for, and who actually bought them.'

'Oh, that's such a relief. It made me afraid they might come to the house and frighten Laura.'

'They shouldn't do that anyway, Tory. I am concerned about this company's debt collection practices, but it's not something you should worry about at the moment.'

'Thank you, Detective.'

'There has been another development, too. Your car has been located.'

Tory stood still, startled. She felt instantly hopeful.

'Oh, that is fantastic. Is it okay?' Tory asked.

'No. Unfortunately, the thieves set fire to the car and completely burned it. We aren't able to get fingerprints from the car, which is why they burn them, of course. At the moment, we still aren't any closer to understanding who stole it.'

How ironic, Tory thought. Providing her fingerprints had been a complete waste of time.

'So, what happens now?'

'I will give you a report saying the car is a write-off. You can give it to your insurance company so they can pay your claim. We will keep searching for the thieves, although I don't hold much hope of us finding them now.'

'Oh. I guess that's it, then,' Tory mumbled.

'The good news is now you've blocked your credit and cancelled the cards, there should be no more debts against you. There may be a few bad debts already incurred that need sorting, such as the one that came up yesterday, then you should be okay.'

'Thank you, Detective. I am quite anxious thinking about what debts might be out there we aren't aware of, but at least it looks more promising.'

'Okay, enjoy the rest of your day,' the detective said as she disconnected the call.

The conversation reassured Tory. She phoned Brent and left a message outlining the information the detective had conveyed.

* * *

Tory was sipping a coffee as she sat looking over her back garden when her mobile phone buzzed. It was Carolyn, calling from work.

'How's it going, girlfriend? Everyone here is worried about you. Even though Frank sent you on leave, he really cares, too.'

'Thanks, Caro. I'll come and talk to Frank on Monday. Give him time to calm down after those guys showed up.'

'Good. Now, why I actually called you is to tell you I am going on a date tonight for Valentine's Day.'

Tory could hear the smile in her voice.

'With Karl?' Tory asked, excited for her friend.

'Yes, with Karl. I relented. He popped into the office this morning and asked me. He is taking me to The Quaff wine bar.'

'That's perfect, Caro. I'm so happy for you. Call me after and tell me everything.'

'Are you doing something special with Brent?'

Tory hesitated. She wanted to do something nice for Brent; however, considering their problems at the moment, she decided a quiet night at home might be the best option. Plus, she couldn't bring herself to ask Gail to babysit again this week.

'I'm going to cook something nice. I bought his favourite scotch today to give him,' Tory said. 'I hope he likes it.'

'He will. Got to go now, girlfriend. Frank's heading this way. Talk later,' Carolyn said, and she hung up.

Over dinner, Tory shared with Brent the news of Caro's date.

'Good on Karl. He's been trying for a while. I saw him at footy training this week, and he asked me if he had any hope. I told him I had no idea,' Brent said with a grin. 'He'll have his work cut out for him in the gift line. I hope he doesn't buy her perfume or flowers.'

'Yeah, true. I am sure Karl will think of something,' Tory said, also smiling.

* * *

Saturday saw Carolyn sitting in Tory's kitchen, coloured pencil in hand, helping Laura colour a picture.

'So how did last night go with Karl?' Tory asked.

Carolyn looked up. 'It went okay. It was a bit awkward, to be honest. Neither of us knew what to say at times.'

'Do you think you will go out with him again?' Tory asked.

'Probably. If he wants to, I will give it another go,' Carolyn said. 'How did you go?'

'We had a nice night. Laura kept us company,' Tory said. She didn't want to say much in front of her daughter.

'No gifts?'

Tory shook her head. 'No. Brent reminded me funds aren't flush right now. His boss offered the opportunity for him to work overtime today, and he accepted.'

Carolyn glanced at the bottle of scotch sitting on the bench and stayed silent.

Tory watched Laura and Carolyn colouring together. Suddenly, she had a flashback to her mother's parting words as Tory was leaving after being kicked out of the house.

'You are always too smart for the rest of us, with your books and big words. Well, not so smart now, are you?' her mother had said.

Harsh words that stung. She was determined not to be that kind of mother to Laura.

* * *

Tory regretted not being able to stay in contact with Glenda, the friend who offered Pricilla a bed to sleep in. Glenda's home was comfortable and safe. Tory would model herself on Glenda, she had decided. This woman looked after her house, worked at a good job, and showed kindness to her friends. Watching Glenda, Pricilla knew this was the life she wanted. Glenda welcomed her for the three weeks it took for the new identity to be posted to the house. The postman arrived with the new identity while Glenda was at work. Pricilla almost felt disappointed when she collected the mail and found the letter addressed to Tory. From that moment, Pricilla ceased to exist.

Tory packed her bag, left a thank-you note on the dining table, and walked out. She worried how hurt Glenda might be by her guest leaving without saying goodbye. Tory didn't feel much of a friend. If she was going to survive, however, she knew that Glenda and anyone from her past must not have any clue what her new name was or where she lived. With her new identity, Tory boarded a train to Sydney, never to return to her childhood town of Port Macquarie.

Tory found the first months in Sydney difficult. She drifted from accommodation to accommodation, staying in cheap boarding homes, lucky if she found a lock on her room's door. She got work in the kitchen of a fast-food place, volunteering for any shifts available. Tory saved a small amount, enough to reliably allow her to pay the rent in the share house she found. Her three housemates worked different shifts, and after work, Tory had the home to herself most of the time.

Tory wanted a better job, to be more like Glenda, and so enrolled in TAFE. Unsure what course she wanted to do, the time of day the classes ran decided the outcome for Tory. She enrolled in a Certificate III of Business Administration because the classes had hours that would allow her to both work and study. Tory enjoyed the course, did well, and on completion, the teacher encouraged her to undertake the Certificate IV level. Study ignited Tory's enthusiasm for learning, something her home life extinguished in her high school years. Weeks before her move to Aloma, Tory was proud to receive a second certificate, this time in financial accounting.

Tory never learned to cook at home, and although she worked in a takeaway food store, she took every opportunity to learn how to cook. She offered to help her housemates when they made meals, gaining skills along the way. In Sydney, she dated a few men. None treated her well, and one day, she took a look around her, assessed the men she attracted, and decided it was time to leave Sydney.

Each day after work, Tory scanned the papers and internet for jobs. She applied for any job she thought she could do that sounded interesting. When Frank called her for an interview, Tory jumped up and down with excitement. They skyped the interview, and on the spot, Frank offered her the job. Within two weeks, Tory made Aloma home, using her meagre savings to lease a small one-bedroom unit.

* * *

'Tory, are you going to the barbeque at the footy club tomorrow? Karl mentioned it,' Carolyn asked, interrupting Tory's reminiscing.

Laura finished her picture and skipped off to her room to play. Sure Laura couldn't hear, Tory responded, 'Ah, I don't think so. Brent hasn't mentioned it. After he finishes overtime again tomorrow, we are going to his parents' for an early dinner … something I am not looking forward to.'

'Have you spoken to them since they learned of your other name?' Carolyn asked.

'Barely. She looked after Laura when she was sick at school, and then when we went out the other night, but she didn't speak more than two words to me. I think she may have actually grimaced when she saw me. Brent said she was sorry for what she said, but I am not sure she actually apologised. Certainly, she hasn't to me. The dinner is supposed to break the ice on the hostilities. It should be a blast,' Tory said, the sarcasm palpable.

* * *

Brent's mates teased him about his mum. *'She still wipe your bum?'* they would ask, laughing at him.

Brent loved her but wished she could take a step back and not interfere with his and Tory's lives quite so much. He'd tried to talk to his mother when Tory fell pregnant.

'Mum, I love Tors and want to marry her. It's not just because she's pregnant.'

'Brent, you hardly know her. She either doesn't know how to look after a home or she's lazy. Neither is good enough for you.'

'Tors is plenty good enough for me, Mum. Please be nice to her.'

'For you, I'll try. Just don't let her get away with being lazy. Once the baby is born, you will want her to pull her weight.'

'Tors works hard, Mum. Her job keeps her busy.'

'We raised you to be a good man, Brent. I hope you are doing the right thing now.'

'I am, Mum. Just imagine, I'm going to be a dad. Can you believe it!' Brent looked at her with a grin splitting his face.

When they announced they were going to be married, he had to ask his father to stop his mother from planning their wedding after she badgered him and Tory with suggestions for the reception and guest list.

Brent was proud of Tory and the restraint she showed. Everyone knew Gail loved him, and being the only son and youngest child apparently meant he could not care for himself. His two older sisters hated his mum doing stuff for him, mostly because they'd like Gail to do it for them, too. The smothering by his mother drove him and Tory to move to Aloma. He wanted a geographical buffer between them and his parents, to prevent his mother calling around too often. His dad didn't smother. Basically, he did what Gail told him to do and kept a low profile in the decision-making stakes.

Brent worried about his and Tory's relationship. While he was angry with Tory, his mother's reaction shocked him. Despite Tory's complaints about Gail, Brent had thought his mother actually liked her. After her reaction to Tory's past identity, he wasn't sure. For his family's sake, Brent realised they needed to get on with each other, so despite the teasing of his mates, Sunday's family dinner was important. Hopefully, Gail would mend her relationship with Tory, or at least make things civil.

* * *

Tory walked Carolyn to the front door.

'I'll see you at work on Monday, girlfriend.' Carolyn leant in to kiss Tory on the cheek.

'If I survive dinner tomorrow night, you will indeed.'

Tory opened the door and looked down. She saw the familiar yellow and white of a plastic courier bag.

'Oh shit, another delivery,' Tory said. She bent to pick up the parcel.

'Maybe the order went in before you cancelled the cards?' Carolyn said.

'I hope so. I better get on the phone to the sender and sort this one out,' Tory sighed as Carolyn gave her a quick hug and walked to her car.

CHAPTER 26

'Come on, Laura. In the car now. We don't want to be late for Gran's,' Tory called.

'Which car, Mum?'

'Dad's truck.'

Tory approached this evening's visit with dread. She understood its importance to Brent. He wanted her to have a good relationship with his mum. Brent continued to be angry with her for not confiding in him about her past. She was desperate for his forgiveness and would suck up a year of dinners with his parents if that was what it took.

They loaded into the truck, and Brent backed it out of the garage. A new and expensive-looking white sports car, parked a few doors away, caught Tory's eye. She glanced at the grill with the three-point emblem of a Mercedes gleaming in the sunlight.

Nice for some, she thought as they drove past.

* * *

Anton watched them leave.

He arrived in Aloma yesterday evening after a gruelling two-day drive. The drive took longer than planned and exhausted him. On arrival, Anton found the best motel in Aloma and checked in, but it barely met his high standards. His suite consisted of a large bedroom with a luxury bathroom. The entrance door led to a small sitting room that backed onto a functional kitchenette containing a small refrigerator stocked with essentials, including a complimentary bottle of champagne. A welcome basket of food sat on the bench. The decor presented walls in muted shades of coffee and brown, with bright orange and emerald-green throw cushions on the beige couch and chair. Several brightly coloured modern art prints hung on the walls.

Anton looked around the room and grunted before picking up the phone. He ordered room service to bring a meal, a bottle of scotch, and a bucket of ice.

The next morning, re-energised after a good night's sleep in the moderately comfortable bed and a large breakfast, Anton made his way to his car and set his Google Maps to the street Pricilla, or Tory as she went by now, lived. He wanted to set eyes on her. He planned to scope the house out for the whole day or as long as it took. On that night, years before, Anton barely caught a glimpse of Pricilla, with her purple hair, running away. He wanted to know what she now looked like.

He parked his car a few houses away from the address and watched. Late morning, a woman emerged from the front door. She wore a hat and walked out of the house with her back to him. As she got into a car parked on the kerb, Anton's view was blocked by a tree on the nature strip, and he didn't get a good look at her. As the car was parked on the street, Anton reasoned it was unlikely to be Tory. Since then, the only movement he observed had been a man – the husband, he assumed – who arrived in a work truck at two o'clock.

A short time later, three people, a man, woman, and child, left by the front door and entered the garage. Adrenaline spiked in his body as he sat taller to improve his view. The woman was of medium height, with a fit, slim figure and short blonde hair. The little girl skipping next to her sported two long pigtails.

What a happy family, he thought bitterly. The truck backed out and drove past him. He caught a brief closer view of the woman sitting in the front seat.

Anton murmured a prayer to his wife. 'Fuck that woman with the perfect family. She makes me sick. God, how I hate her. She is going to pay. I'm at the end of my life, probably living on borrowed time, but I will make her pay, Sophia, I promise, if it's the last thing I do.'

The surge of hatred he felt now didn't surprise him. Over the past seven years, it had been his sole goal to find and punish her. He'd wanted to get a better look at Tory, to make sure he could recognise her when he took revenge. Anton was undecided about how he might end Tory's life. He knew one thing for sure: he would look her in the eye and she would understand her time was up. The past had caught up with her.

She looked different to how he imagined her. For the past seven years, he had grown a picture of this woman in his mind. He imagined she was a junkie. That she lived a gypsy life, stealing to keep alive, a scum-of-the-earth type. The woman he just laid eyes on looked middle-class. Well-dressed and responsible. It hit him with a jolt; he realised he was disappointed. He wanted her to have lived a hard life, not have had it easy.

The rage Anton maintained toward the two intruders remained strong. His beautiful Sophia, taken from him twice. After she passed, his one solace had been talking to her. He focused on the Fabergé box. Knowing it held her ashes, he could speak to it, share his thoughts with Sophia, profess his undying love.

After the ashes were stolen, and thrown to the tip no less, Anton felt a gaping hole open in his heart. To remedy the wound, he contracted workers to build him a special garden at his house, in honour of his wife. He filled it with plants Sophia loved. A beautifully crafted bench sat at one end so he could visit the area, and he hoped to connect with his Sophia's spirit again. But it didn't work. He sat on the bench, unable to bring himself to speak. How could he explain to Sophia he let her ashes be thrown away? Words would not come. He had let her down. Nothing would right this wrong. Revenge was all he had left.

Anton looked at his shaking hands. His knuckles were white as they gripped the steering wheel. He took a deep breath, started the car, and slowly drove back to his motel. He needed a few more of those scotches this afternoon.

* * *

Brent parked the truck in his parents' front drive. Laura leapt out and ran to the door.

'Granny, Granny, we're here,' she called.

Gail opened the door and bent down to hug Laura. She looked past her to Brent and Tory.

'Good afternoon. Glad you could come,' she greeted them.

Tory understood today was important to her marriage. The outcome could guide the direction her marriage took. Apprehensive, her stomach churned. Tory recognised she didn't have family relationship skills. She didn't have much of a role model in her own childhood, but she wanted badly to be a good mother. While she was pregnant, afraid she wouldn't know what to do, Tory convinced Brent to attend parenting classes with her. While the classes definitely helped, Gail always left her with a sense of inadequacy. Gail, who successfully raised three children, could always point out some alternate way of doing whatever Tory did. She'd never be good enough in Gail's eyes.

* * *

Brent looked at his mother.

I hope she tries to be nice today, he silently prayed.

His family meant everything to him, his parents, his wife and daughter. Still angry and hurt with Tory, last night, after shutting his eyes, he imagined his life without her and Laura. He realised he couldn't live life without them. He had to get over Tory's secret. He wanted to provide the love and stability she didn't have growing up. Discovering Tory's past made him realise how hard she worked to be a good mother and wife, and he desperately wanted his parents to reconcile with her. He didn't want to have to choose between his parents and Tory, nor did he want to continue to walk a tightrope of emotions between the two.

Gail welcomed Tory and Brent into the house. Out of the corner of his eye, Brent was relieved to see Gail grab Tory's hand

and give it a squeeze. He didn't hear what Gail said to Tory, but she nodded and gave Gail a quick hug before they both walked to the kitchen, where Gordon was telling Laura a story about chickens.

Gail put on a delicious lunch. They sat and ate. The adults happily let Laura lead most of the conversation in her five-year-old grown-up way. At times, the strain of everyone being too nice, trying too hard, resulted in an awkward silence. On those occasions, Laura, loving the attention, soon jumped in with some anecdote from school, usually a complaint about one of the schoolboys.

Whatever it takes, he thought.

'So, Brent, how's pre-season going?' Gordon asked as he put his fork down to pick up his beer.

'It's good. The boys are training well. I'm going to have some competition to get into the firsts this year. I hope I can have a few good practice games to consolidate my spot, but there are young guns nipping at my heels.'

'You'll be right. You still have six or so weeks before the season starts. You'll be fit by then,' Gordon said.

'We have a fundraising evening this week, Tuesday. It's probably where they will ask you to volunteer in the canteen again, Tory,' Brent said.

'I don't mind doing the canteen. It's always a bit of fun, and everyone appreciates us all taking a turn.'

'Now you have Nan's car, will you need us to help pick up Laura from after-school care?' Gail asked. 'I don't mind. In fact, I'd love to do it now and then.'

'Thanks for your help over the past few weeks,' Tory said.

'Things can go back to normal now. Fingers crossed I can go back to work and get back to our old routine.'

'Well, we are always here. Just ask if you need,' Gail said. 'Hopefully, you get your job back, so Brent doesn't have to keep doing overtime.'

Brent anticipated Tory's sharp look toward him. He gave a quick shake of his head and offered her a discreet apologetic smile.

The afternoon ended with no raised voices. Relieved, Brent got into the truck to leave. He put his head back in the seat and breathed out. Brent looked over at Tory and put his hand on her leg.

'Thanks for today, Tors. Mum seemed to be making an effort. She didn't say anything too off, did she?'

'No, it was a good day. Still some tension, but nothing like the last time.'

Brent smiled in relief.

CHAPTER 27

Tory returned home after driving Laura to school and called Frank.

'Hi, Frank. It's Tory.'

'Morning, Tory,' Frank said, his voice sounding bright and cheery.

'Frank, I want to say again how sorry I am for last week. I've spoken to the police, and they've been in contact with the debt collection company. They understand there's a dispute about who incurred the debt, and they've put the debt collection on hold. No one should be chasing me for payments. Everything else has been frozen. So, hopefully, I'm on the way to getting my ID back. Unfortunately, it seems a long, slow process,' Tory told him.

'And so you want to come back to work, yes?' Frank asked.

'Yes, please. Is that alright?'

'Okay. You can come back tomorrow. I don't want to see any more heavies coming to the office, though.'

'You and me both.'

Tory breathed a sigh of relief and sent off a quick text to Carolyn.

Frank said ok come back! C U tomorrow.

For the first time in weeks, Tory felt lighthearted. After returning from his parents' yesterday, she and Brent made love. They'd missed each other after letting fear and anger cloud their passion and love, creating a barrier between them. Last night, some of that anger and fear seemed to dissipate, and they rediscovered their desire for each other. As she lay next to him afterwards, she smiled and stroked her finger along his body. If this was what they called make-up sex, she would fight with him more often.

Later in the day, Tory checked the mailbox. Inside, she found a handwritten note, the paper folded in half, with no envelope. Tory unfolded it and read the one-line message.

Tory Packenham you owe a debt you WILL pay!

How odd. Why did the debt collectors go to the trouble of coming to her home and putting the note in the mailbox when they said they'd put things on hold? When she showed Brent later, he, too, was confused.

'Maybe they got annoyed by the police telling them they need to wait till the fraud stuff is sorted out before they chase the debt?' he said.

'It doesn't seem very professional,' Tory said.

'Make sure you keep the doors locked. I am glad you are going back to work tomorrow, so you're not home alone.'

* * *

Carolyn arrived at Tory's house the following evening just as Tory finished putting a freshly iced cake onto a plate. Carolyn was driving with them to the football fundraiser.

'When Karl asked me to go, I knew you guys would be there, so I said yes,' Carolyn said. 'Karl has to get there early, and I didn't want to arrive alone, so thanks for offering to give me a lift.'

'Anytime,' Tory said.

'Did you make that cake?' Carolyn asked, watching Tory wrestle cling wrap over it.

'I had to do something. I am worried the footy guys are going to blame me for our financial situation. They're aware Brent did the overtime last week, and I was out of work for a few days, not that I didn't get paid for those days, but it looks bad.'

'Don't be silly, Tors,' Carolyn said. 'They only think you got robbed and your ID nicked. They're not aware of the other shit that's gone down. They love you. Stop being paranoid.'

'I don't know. They love Brent more than me. I don't reckon they'd stick by me if they realised I caused problems for Brent.'

'Rubbish, girlfriend. They love you equally. Stop putting yourself down. They reckon you are great, helping out all the time, doing the canteen shifts … baking cakes.'

'Okay, you win,' Tory laughed as she and Carolyn followed Laura and Brent through the kitchen to the garage. 'Let's go.'

The evening was fun. Tory sat at one of the trestle tables in the hall and watched with amusement as Karl hovered around Carolyn, bringing her drinks and plates of food, flirting and generally monopolising her.

'Karl's working a bit hard, although I can see Carolyn is

enjoying the attention,' Tory said, giving Brent a nudge with her elbow.

'Yeah. Karl told me he is keen on her. I told him not to give up,' Brent said with a grin.

Tory noticed that while Brent's mates were enjoying his company, they and their partners included her in the banter. She felt comfortable with this group of people and appreciated how family-oriented the club was, too. Laura and the other children in attendance sat at a table covered in stencils, paper, and colouring pencils to keep them entertained, and food to keep them quiet.

This is actually the life I want, Tory reflected. *I'll do anything to keep it.*

* * *

The next morning, Brent kissed his girls goodbye and walked out to his truck to head to work. His mind ran over the time-table of jobs for today. It would be a busy day, with three sites to sort out. He shut the front door and noticed there was a sheet of paper sticking out from the mailbox. He deviated in that direction and pulled out the folded paper. His face paled as he read it.

'Fucking hell,' he breathed as he rushed back inside the house, waving the note.

'Tors, you had better read this. It was in the mailbox.'

She took it from him and read:

Enjoying your life? Want to end up in the tip? Watch your back!

'Oh my God. It's him! Shit, that other note must've been from him too, not the debt collectors,' Tory said. 'He was here, at our house!'

'Shhh, keep your voice down so Laura doesn't hear you,' Brent whispered. 'How the hell did he find you? Even though you have a different name, he still found our home.'

'I don't know,' Tory said. She sounded frantic.

'Did he do the robbery, do you think?' Brent asked.

Tory paused for a moment.

'I doubt it. He didn't know where I lived. He didn't find me in Sydney just after I left, so how could he find me here?'

'I don't know, but maybe he arranged to rob the place to make you feel scared, and the ID stuff to mess with you?'

'It doesn't seem right, Brent. If he knew where we lived, it's more likely he would have hurt me that night, not robbed us.'

'True. Then, how?'

'The police found out about my other name from the fingerprints. Maybe he got information off them or their database. Maybe he has a source with the police. Someone he could pay for information on me.'

'I should've installed those security cameras. What does he even look like?' Brent said.

Tory shrugged her shoulders. 'We can't go around running away from every old guy we see. What are we going to do, Brent?'

Brent could see the fear in Tory's eyes. *Damn that bastard. Was she safe? What about Laura?*

'I'm not sure. If he has people in the police, we can't really go to them, at least not yet. Let's just go to work for now, as normal. Make sure you're never alone. Call me when you're ready to leave work, and if I'm not home yet, you can go somewhere else till I am. Okay?'

'Yes. Thanks. I'll call you.'

Brent felt reassured. As long as Tory was not alone, she should be safe.

'When we get home tonight, we can jump online and see what we can find about this guy. What's his name again?'

'Anton,' Tory said.

'There must be something we can find out about him. Maybe there's a recent photo, who knows?' Brent said. 'I need to get to a job now. You take Laura now to the early drop-off at school and go to work. We can talk more tonight.'

The note in the mailbox had freaked him out. Was Tory being hunted? It felt like it.

* * *

Anton liked routine. It helped him start his day in a positive frame of mind. The motel's policy of breakfast served only in the restaurant, with no room service, made him bloody shitty when he tried to order breakfast to his room on the first morning. He complained to the person on the end of the internal phone. Then, when he realised he wasn't going to win this one, he slammed the receiver down so hard he jarred his hand.

'Damn hick town,' he cursed.

He stomped to the lift and pushed the ground-floor button.

Surprisingly, Anton found he didn't mind the early bustle of motel guests chatting over breakfast and waitstaff expertly serving tables. Every morning at eight o'clock sharp, he sat at his table.

The staff were efficient; he gave them that much. 'Thank you, Rose,' he said to one of them, noting her name on the badge worn on her shirt pocket, as she brought his cappuccino and the local newspaper the minute he sat at his table.

'Good morning, sir. Your eggs will be ready shortly.'

Without having to ask, two poached eggs on toast would arrive ten minutes after he sat, and as he finished reading the paper, a second coffee, his heart-starter as he liked to call it, a strong macchiato, would be placed in front of him. He ensured such service with the hundred-dollar tip and instructions given on that first morning.

With enough money, you can always get what you want, he thought, pleased with himself. He smiled with self-satisfaction while sipping his cappuccino. He imagined the stress Tory would be experiencing now.

He enjoyed toying with her.

Making her squirm for a while.

Over the next few days, he planned to track her. See what she got up to. Anton was grateful for Graham's call. He wondered what Tory had done to come to the attention of the police, why her fingerprints had been put into the system. When he saw her yesterday, she didn't look like a person who'd committed a crime. Looks can be misleading, he knew. She could have been out on bail, but it didn't seem to fit with what he saw. It didn't matter to him one way or the other. He had finally found her, and she would atone for her actions.

He didn't have much left in life, and this moment would be his final act of revenge. He'd spent the past seven years imagining, in all manner of ways, how he would kill her. Now the time had arrived, he really did need to take a step back from the gratifying, cruel deaths he imagined and take a simple and effective approach. He just wasn't sure which way to go. Anton thought about the gun, hidden in his room. It was his best option; however, a shooting might implicate him, or at least cause an investigation. Perhaps he could arrange another car accident?

He couldn't decide.

No rush. He was enjoying himself. He could suffer the motel. The restaurant chef cooked a good meal, and they kept an impressive wine list. He didn't mind staying a bit longer. He finished his breakfast with a short glass of water, then stood and walked to the lift to take him back to his room to get his car keys. He hummed to himself as he pushed the lift button. He looked forward to following Tory today.

CHAPTER 28

Tory tucked Laura into bed and returned to the dining room, where Brent was sitting at the computer.

'I put Anton Solo in the search box. Look what comes up,' Brent said as he nudged the screen in her direction.

Tory leaned over his shoulder and peered at the screen. There were a few references to Anton. 'I remember that one,' Tory said as she pointed to a news headline announcing farmer compensation for the withdrawal of tobacco-growing licences.

'Remember, I told you he got a payout?'

'Yeah, and this one is about his son being killed in a boat accident a few years ago,' said Brent, hovering the computer mouse over another headline.

'Here is one about the son in jail,' Tory said. 'Look. It has a photo, Anton and his two sons.'

'That photo would be eight or ten years old. Keep searching for a more recent one.'

'Add Port Macquarie into the search, see if that locates something more recent,' suggested Tory.

And there it was. A photo taken two years ago, of Anton

standing next to the local under-fifteens representative football team, coach and players. The headline screamed: *Local Supporter Donates to City Soccer Future.*

Tory looked at the photo.

'Wow. In my head, he was bigger and meaner.'

'He's plenty mean enough,' Brent said.

'True, but he looks like an old man. He's not tall, he's bent over, and he's bald. Look, he even carries a cane!'

'Well, he's still dangerous, Tory.'

'Unless he's moved in the past two years, it looks as if he still lives in Port Macquarie. I wonder if he's in the same mansion.'

'It doesn't matter much,' said Brent. 'He's in Aloma now. That's what we have to worry about.'

'Is he on his own? Could he have people working for him here, too?'

'I'm not sure. He could do. They would be dangerous people if he did.'

'What are we going to do? Should we go to the police?'

'Perhaps not. The letters only sound threatening because of what you did to Anton, and what you assume he did to your friend.'

'I'm sure he killed Jordie,' Tory said, agitated.

'This Jordie guy, I can hear it in your voice … he was more than a mate, wasn't he?'

Tory's bottom lip trembled, and she looked sad.

'Brent, I told you Jordie was my best friend. He was also the first person, and the only one other than you, I slept with.

* * *

The houses on the street were lit up, except for the one Pricilla and Jordie walked toward. Jordie noticed yesterday there were no bins on the street in front of this home.

'I reckon the owners are away,' he told her. 'Let's celebrate your birthday in style.'

Pricilla turned sixteen today. Her mother forgot, or at least didn't mention it that afternoon when Pricilla returned from school. Pricilla dropped her schoolbag in her room, threw her school uniform on the floor, and slipped on a pair of ripped jeans and a T-shirt before walking back out. She met Jordie at the skate rink, where they hung out till the sky turned dark.

'Okay, time to go.' Jordie grabbed her hand and led her through the streets.

The house was in the middle of a neat street lined with large and expensive-looking homes. They walked down the side of the property and quietly opened the gate leading to the backyard. At the rear door, Jordie pulled a hammer and towel from the backpack he carried, and as he held the towel against the small window next to the door, he gave a quick tap with the hammer. The glass shattered and tinkled as it fell to the ground. Jordie reached his arm through the window and unlocked the door from the inside.

'Too easy.' Jordie smiled as they stepped inside. He switched on his torch.

Although all the blinds were closed, they stayed in the rooms facing the back of the property in case light from their torches showed through any gaps.

Pricilla headed to the kitchen while Jordie raced up the stairs.

The fridge was mostly empty, but in the freezer section, Pricilla found a pack of chocolate muffins.

'Whoo-hoo, happy birthday to me.'

The muffins would go with the scotch she found in another cupboard. She sat them on the kitchen bench and looked up to see Jordie with a big grin on his face, walking toward her, holding something behind his back.

'I got you a birthday present. Want to see it?'

'Yes, please.'

Jordie whipped out his hand, and in it was a khaki busboy cap with a tan leather strap across the front.

'I love it!' Pricilla said as she grabbed it off him and set it on her head. 'How's it look?'

'Beautiful, like you.'

Pricilla threw her arms around him, and they kissed. Suddenly, there was electricity between them. She pulled back and looked at Jordie. He nodded and led her by the hand to an upstairs bedroom where they had sex. It was her first time.

The cap reminded Pricilla of that special night. She wore it everywhere, although at school, she kept it in her backpack. One day, months later, Pricilla reached into her backpack after school and realised the cap was not there. With a jolt, she remembered sitting it on her bed as she got ready for school. One of her mother's creepy guys had arrived, so she grabbed her backpack and left quickly. She must have forgotten to pack her cap.

'Shit.' Pricilla ran all the way home.

She flew through the front door and into her room. The unmade bed taunted her. The cap wasn't there.

'Mum,' she yelled. Pricilla rushed to the kitchen where her mother sat, a joint wedged between her fingers.

'Mum, did you take my cap?'

Her mother looked up, eyes bleary.

'Good afternoon to you too, Lady Muck.'

'Mum, my hat. What did you do with it?'

Her mother shrugged and looked at the joint between her fingers. Suddenly, it struck Pricilla. Her mother had traded her cap for the joint.

'How could you? It was mine,' Pricilla screamed.

'Nuffin's yours in my 'ouse.'

Pricilla turned and ran back to her room. She threw herself on her bed and sobbed.

* * *

'Your first time, huh? Should I be worried?' Tory had never mentioned who she'd first slept with, and he felt a twinge of jealousy.

'He's dead, Brent. What do you think?'

'Of course. That was dumb of me. Sorry.' Brent felt like an idiot and changed the subject. 'You said they recorded Jordie's death as an accident. The police won't believe you when you tell them Anton killed him. So then, it's also unlikely they'll take what you say now about Anton seriously. Also, if Anton has a friend in the police, we can't guess how that might influence things.'

'You're right. His contacts might cause us problems, too.'

'I've been thinking,' Brent said after a moment. 'Anton won't know what you look like now, will he? You said you changed your appearance when you moved to Sydney.'

'Yes. I had purple hair back then.'

'You have that bunch of flowers I gave you as your Facebook profile photo, and you never post pictures of yourself or Laura, so there should be no way for him to access a photo, right?'

'That's true. What are you suggesting?'

'You're probably safe if he doesn't have a current picture of you, at least for the time being.'

'He knows where we live, Brent. It won't take him long to see me coming or going from the house.'

'All I'm saying is we probably have a little space to stay safe.'

Tory nodded, leaning against him. 'I hope so. I just don't know what's the best thing to do.'

'Let's chill for now. See how things pan out for a bit. We can play it safe by making sure you always have someone around you, that you're never alone.'

Suddenly, Brent looked at Tory. She could sense a change in him and looked into his eyes, wondering what was going through his mind.

'You know, while we're on the internet, do you want to find out if your mother and brother are still alive? I can help you search,' he asked with caution.

Tory froze. The question was unexpected. Did she want to know? She was certain she wanted nothing to do with her mother. Her poor parenting disgusted her. It made Tory bitter to recall the trauma she grew up surrounded by. In her mind, there were no excuses. Her mother didn't deserve any sort of relationship with her, and she wanted nothing to do with that woman. She certainly didn't want her anywhere near Laura.

Her brother, Sam, on the other hand, held a special place in her heart. Sam's care and support when she was young made her life back then bearable. In fact, without Sam, Tory probably wouldn't be here now. Tory wished he could have stuck around until she was older. He hurt her badly when he disappeared. At the time, it felt almost like he died, and she was both sad and angry with him. A part of her wanted to punch him; the other part wanted to ask him why he abandoned her. She was afraid of the answer he might give to her questions. Still, despite her fear, she did want to find out where he was now.

'I don't know, Brent. I am frightened it might take the lid off something we can't put back on. It might cause damage to what we have here. I wouldn't mind knowing what Sam is doing, though. Can we leave it for a while? Let me sleep on it, please?'

Brent released a deep breath, relieved Tory hadn't snapped his head off when he asked the question. Tory's family was a curiosity for him. From what she told him, they seemed very dysfunctional. However, he wondered if her teenage perspective would change if she spoke to them now. It was obvious Tory was cut up by her upbringing, and he wondered if finding her family might give her some form of closure. He leant in and gave her a quick kiss on the cheek.

'Of course, Tors. Happy to help when you are ready.'

CHAPTER 29

Tory spent a restless night, unable to sleep. Early the next morning, as the first rays of sunlight flickered through the curtains, she rolled over to face Brent, who woke as she spoke.

'Brent, I've been thinking. Seven years ago, to get away from Anton, I changed my name and moved. If it wasn't for the robbery, he'd still have no idea where I am. What if we did it again?'

'What? Change our names?' Brent propped himself up on an elbow and looked at Tory.

'Yes, register for new names and move to Queensland. It'd only be for a few years until he dies of old age. We'd return after he died.'

'What about my job, mum and dad?'

'We'd need to start again with our jobs. Tell your parents it would only be for a few years with no contact … or maybe we'd work out a way for them to make contact with our new names.'

'What if something happens to my parents while we are away? I'd need to leave the footy guys. Laura would need to go to a new school. She wouldn't understand.'

'It's something to consider, Brent.'

'I get that, Tors, but you know what? We can't run forever.

Anton finding you proved that. While you say it may only be a few years, what if he lived to be a hundred? Laura would be an adult. That's too long. We'd need to give up too much. What if we moved only for something else to happen that revealed your alias? Do we move again and again?'

'I don't know, Brent. I'm just worried about you and Laura,' Tory said. She eased a curl of hair off his face with her finger.

'No, it's too much, Tors. We need to sort this here and now. Whatever happens, we must stop him coming after you.' Brent got out of bed and walked to the shower.

'I'm afraid of what that might look like,' Tory said quietly as she watched him go.

* * *

The next afternoon, Tory stopped the orange car out the front of Laura's after-school care centre. At the end of the school day, a teacher walked the children the short way from the school to the centre. The facility consisted of a cluster of old demountable classrooms. Several offices had been modelled in the back of one building. The yard around the buildings, where the children played when the weather was fine, was fenced off to provide security. Tory saw a game of tag being played with lots of excited children yelling.

'Good afternoon.' She smiled at the woman supervising the children.

'Afternoon, Tory. Oh, Janice has asked me to ask if you can pop in and see her before you pick up Laura today. She's in her office.'

'No worries,' Tory said. She turned toward the centre director's office and stepped into the doorway. The small office was filled with a large desk covered in paperwork. Craft items given to her by the children lined the edge of the desk nearest to her. The director, a woman of fifty years, with grey hair styled in a short bob, wore casual clothing, jeans and a floral blouse. She sat at the desk, working on her computer.

'Hi, Janice. You wanted to see me?'

'Ah, yes, Tory, thanks for coming,' she said as she looked up from her computer. 'I wanted to tell you, Laura's grandfather arrived to pick her up an hour ago. He's not on the authorised list for pick-ups, so I didn't let him take her. I hope that didn't cause any problems?' Janice asked, her voice filled with concern.

'Oh,' Tory said, surprised. 'He wasn't supposed to get her. His wife, Gail, usually does the pick-up if I need help. It's odd. There must be a miscommunication somewhere.' Tory shrugged.

'That's alright. He took it well. Laughed and said he must've gotten confused. He left straight away.'

'Okay, thanks for telling me.' Tory walked back to where the children played and waved for Laura to come. She ran over, picked up her schoolbag from the shelf, and followed Tory to the car. Laura chatted happily about her day on the trip home.

When Brent returned that evening, Tory questioned him.

'Did you ask your dad to pick up Laura today? Janice from the centre said she had to turn him away when he tried to pick her up because he wasn't on the approved access list.'

'No. I didn't ask him.'

'Can you call Gordon and ask why he wanted to pick her up, please? It's not like him to do that. Maybe something was wrong with your mum, and Gordon thought he needed to do the care run for her?'

After speaking to his parents, Brent walked into the kitchen, where Tory was preparing dinner.

'Tors, Dad says he didn't go to the centre. Neither did Mum. They haven't left the house all day.'

'That's odd. Who could have …' Tory let the words fade as an ugly realisation hit her. 'Do you think it was Anton?' she whispered. A sick feeling rose in her stomach.

'That bastard, it better not have been.' Brent's body tensed with anger.

'I'll kill him if he touches Laura,' said Tory, her eyes narrowed.

'Let's calm down. Not get too far ahead of ourselves.' Brent took a deep, calming breath.

'I need to call Janice, get her to describe the guy.' Tory reached for her mobile.

'Hey, Tors, it can wait till tomorrow. You don't want to disturb her after hours. She might not appreciate it, especially when they did the right thing and didn't let him take Laura.'

'I guess you are right. I'm just anxious to find out if it was Anton. He wouldn't hurt a little girl, would he?'

'Frankly, Tory, I don't know what he might do. From what you said, he is pretty ruthless.'

'Shit. Now I'm ten times more worried.'

'Tomorrow when you drop Laura at school, call into the centre and see if they can describe the guy.'

'Yes, and I will emphasise that no one else is to take her home. Thank God they stuck to the rules this time.'

CHAPTER 30

At school the next morning, Laura bounded off to play with her friends, and Tory walked next door to the centre to speak to Janice.

'Good morning,' Tory said as she walked into the director's office. 'Do you have a minute?'

'Of course. How can I help?'

'Can you please describe the man who tried to pick up Laura yesterday? Her grandfather denies being here.'

'Oh dear. I am sorry, Tory. I didn't set eyes on him. It was one of the staff who told me. She is not in today, so I can't ask her. She told me she observed the man to make sure he left and said he got into a white Mercedes parked on the street.'

'Can you call her? When will she be at work next?'

'The interaction should be on video from our security cameras. When you come back for Laura this afternoon, I can have the footage ready to view if you like?'

Cameras are good, Tory thought. *I'll be able to get a good look at who it was.*

'Awesome. That is fantastic. Thank you, Janice. I'll see you later.'

All day at work, Tory's mind kept returning to someone trying to take Laura. The white car he got into pricked something in her mind.

Why does that sound familiar?

Damn!

It hit her. She'd seen a new white Merc at the end of their street a few days ago when they were driving to Brent's parents. She wasn't sure, but Tory thought she may have seen it yesterday too, driving behind her when she pulled into work. Was she being paranoid?

On edge to view the video and unable to concentrate at work, Tory left the office early and arrived at the centre well before the usual pick-up time.

'Come in,' Janice said, waving Tory toward her office. 'I accessed the video for yesterday, and it's set to when the gentleman arrived for Laura. Have a seat here, and I'll start it.'

Janice tilted the computer screen on her desk toward Tory so she could get a better view and pressed play.

Tory's eyes focused on the screen. The video was a little grainy. It showed parents arriving to pick up children. The children running to pick up their backpacks and waving to staff as they walked out. The staff speaking to parents and children alike. Then, there he was. An older man. No hair. Bald. He walked hunched, leaning on a cane.

Tory gasped. It felt ghoulish watching him. She tried to conceal the anger that rose in her. The gall. It was Anton. She was sure. She watched as he spoke to a female staff member. She shook her head, as if to offer an apology. Anton then shrugged his shoulders, turned, and walked away along the footpath. The video showed the staff member walking to the gate and looking along the road, where she presumably observed him get into his car.

'Do you know him?' Janice asked. She looked anxious.

Tory had to come up with something fast. She didn't want to identify Anton to Janice. She took a deep breath.

'Er, yes, I am afraid so. He's a nutty neighbour,' she said. 'We don't need to report him to the police. I'm in contact with his son. I will talk to him to make sure the old guy doesn't try it again. Whatever you do, don't let Laura go with anyone other than me, Brent, or Gail.'

'Of course, Tory. Our security is very important.'

'Yesterday proved that, and I'm very grateful. Thank you for showing me this video. It really helped.'

'My pleasure.' Janice smiled and sounded relieved.

Tory found Laura in the playground. Tory's mind worked overtime as she drove home. What on earth was Anton up to? He was happy enough to leave when asked, rather than cause a scene. What would he have done if the centre had let him take Laura? What would they have done when Laura told them he was not her grandfather? Tory doubted Laura would have gotten into the car with him. She hoped not, anyway. As she drove, her eyes glanced up to the rear-vision mirror and to Laura in the back seat.

'Laura, if someone tries to pick you up from school, or the centre, if you don't know them, you won't go with them, will you?'

'No, Mummy, not even if they offer me ice cream,' Laura said.

'That's good. I'll always make sure someone you know picks you up, okay?'

'Yeah, okay, Mummy. Can we get ice cream now?' Laura asked, always hopeful.

'Not today, darling. We need to get home.'

Laura pouted and then recommenced playing with the doll she held in her hands.

Later that evening, after they'd put Laura to bed, Brent and Tory sat in the lounge room and discussed the video.

'I can't believe he had the nerve to go to the centre and ask to take her. Tory, what sort of creep is he?'

Tory could sense him bristling with tension.

'I don't have a clue. I wonder if he really wanted to take her, or was he trying to scare us, send a message?'

'Well, message received. I'm going to punch his lights out.' Brent clenched and unclenched his fists.

'Do you think it's time we took this to the police?'

'I don't know. He didn't actually take Laura, and he may never have intended to. If the centre staff had let him take her or offered to call one of us, he may have walked away. He's done nothing wrong, technically. I'm not sure he could even be considered as stalking you yet. You haven't noticed him following you for sure, just the once parked on our street,' Brent said.

'I guess not. I must say I'm feeling pretty uneasy. He's crossed a line by involving Laura, even if it was just a taunt.'

'Crossed big time! I want to find him and put my fist into his face. Then he'll understand not to play games with us or our daughter.'

'Brent, don't do that. I can just imagine him laughing at me when you get arrested for attacking him. With you locked up, he could hassle me even more.'

'Tory, I don't know. I think he's playing for keeps on this. I'm not sure how this is going to end. Perhaps we do need to confront him?'

Tory shrugged. 'I don't want to make things worse.'

'Well, one thing's for sure. I'm not going away next week. I don't care about the overtime. I'll tell the boss I can't go. He won't be happy, but he can find someone else to spend the week at Tumut.'

'Oh, Brent,' Tory said. 'I'm sorry. I am glad you're not going, though. I'm starting to feel frightened.'

'We'll figure it out, Tors,' Brent said as he gave her a protective hug.

* * *

Tory woke to find a text on her phone from Detective Blunt.

Is it ok if I drop around early this morning before work to catch up?

She responded with a thumbs-up emoji.

'Hey, Brent, wake up. Detective Blunt's dropping around this morning. Better get dressed.'

'I wonder if she has any new information on who did the robbery? You still okay with saying nothing about Anton?'

'Yes, although I might question her about stalking. Ask her if there is something worth doing to stop it.'

'Okay, just be careful what you say. I want to figure out what we are going to do about him first before we mention it to the police.'

The detective arrived as Tory was cutting up a sandwich for Laura's lunch. Laura was in her room getting ready for school.

Brent brought the detective into the kitchen.

'Morning, Detective Blunt,' Tory said. 'You don't mind if I keep making lunches while you talk?'

'Of course. Thanks for seeing me this early. I figured with you both working, this would be the most convenient time.'

'What do you have for us, Detective?' Brent asked.

'Not a lot, I'm afraid. The news is, with respect to the robbery, we have no leads, and I wanted to tell you, while the case will remain open, we're not going to be actively investigating further, unless some new information comes to light.'

'So that's it. What about the ID theft?' Tory said.

'Our fraud team in Sydney is still working on that. Yours and a lot of other stolen identities are possibly linked to a known syndicate. Police will keep chasing this, but from your point of view, it's not likely going to mean much. Now, as you have frozen your credit, and the bank has updated your cards, there shouldn't be any new issues for you. If we apprehend them, you might have to go to court as a witness.'

'Right. That all seems so unsatisfactory, somehow,' Brent said, shaking his head.

Detective Blunt's face reflected empathy. 'I am sorry I can't do more.'

'Detective, do you mind if I ask you something for a friend?' Tory said.

'Sure.'

'A friend told me she thought someone was following her. She thinks he dropped a note in her mailbox, saying he was keeping an eye on her. He hasn't physically done anything to her, but she is a bit worried. Is there anything she can do to stop him?'

'Your friend can apply to the police for an AVO, an Apprehended Violence Order. The court can order an AVO if your friend can demonstrate a reasonable fear of violence or harassment from the person.'

'The AVOs, do they work?'

'The AVO can say the man can't come within a certain distance of your friend, including the street she lives or works in. If he does, he can be charged with breaching the order. In terms of your question, do they work?' Detective Blunt shrugged her shoulders. 'There are many examples of people who do breach the orders. Some get arrested. Some do actual harm to the victim in that last contact. It's difficult to say. They are certainly a deterrent.'

'Okay, thanks for that,' Tory said.

'If your friend is worried, she should talk to the police. Encourage her to come to the station or call us. Someone can talk to her about it,' Detective Blunt offered as she got up to leave.

'Thanks for dropping around and giving us the update, Detective,' said Brent as he walked her out.

'Well, that wasn't very helpful,' he announced when he returned to the kitchen. 'Can you ask Caro to come around tonight to keep you company while I'm at footy training?'

'I asked her yesterday, and she'll come home with me after work.'

'Good. Talk later,' Brent said as he headed out the door with Laura in tow.

* * *

Tory picked Laura up from care and met Carolyn at their home.

'It's Caro!' Laura said with an excited squeal. As soon as Tory stopped the car, she jumped out and ran to Carolyn.

'Hi, precious,' Carolyn said, giving her a hug.

Laura dragged Carolyn by the hand into the house.

'Come and look at my room. I have the perfume sitting on my dresser. I use it every morning.'

Carolyn dutifully discussed with Laura her room, her dolls, and when they were going to make more perfume before leaving her and wandering into the dining room, where Tory was pouring two glasses of wine.

'So, girlfriend,' she said, taking a glass from Tory. 'Why am I here? What's the issue with you and Laura being home alone?'

'Oh, Caro, things are getting pretty fucked up.'

Tory shared how Anton went to the centre and the notes he left in her mailbox.

They chatted about other things for a while but returned to the topic of Anton when Brent got back from training.

'He's obviously toying with you. He must be mad,' Carolyn said. She was incredulous anyone could threaten Laura.

'He's obviously out of his mind,' Brent said. 'He can't seem to let go of what happened all those years ago.'

Tory dropped her head and whispered, 'I'm afraid he's dangerous.'

'Do you think he is on his own in his mad quest to upset you, or is someone helping him?' Carolyn asked, looking at her friend, concern in her eyes.

'Who knows? We haven't seen evidence of anyone else,' Brent said.

'I'll be here for you both anytime. Brent, you don't have to worry. Between us, we can make sure Tory and Laura are never alone. Hopefully, he won't try anything when one of us is here.'

'Thanks, Caro,' Tory said. She looked at her friend with gratitude.

The three sat in silence as each considered what might happen next.

CHAPTER 31

The engagement party promised to be fun. Since they received their invitation from their footy club friends three weeks earlier, Tory had been looking forward to an evening of fun and lighthearted conversation to take her mind off things. As she stood beside Carolyn, wine glass in hand, and one eye on Laura playing with other children in the corner of the room, she watched the happy couple, Sean and Leanne, greet guests arriving at the clubrooms. Sparkling helium balloons wishing the couple a happy engagement floated around the ceiling of the clubroom, and music played from a boom box. Tory turned to Carolyn, who looked stunning as usual. She wore long tan boots and a short, figure-hugging dress made of cream lace. The outfit accentuated her height and her curves. Tory felt good in her pretty summer dress and low heels, too. Hers was a more functional outfit, something she could chase down Laura in if she misbehaved.

'They look happy. It's so lovely. And, yes, we are at another function at the clubrooms,' Tory said, her cheerful voice matching her mood.

'It's pretty much a mandatory venue for these things if you are a club member,' Carolyn acknowledged with a laugh.

'Well, it has a good dance floor and plenty of room. Keep that in mind when you and Karl take the next step.'

'Whoa, slow that boat down, girlfriend. We are nowhere near that stage of our relationship.'

Tory stiffened.

'Oh, look who just walked in, dragon lady and her husband,' she said as Brent's parents arrived.

'Stick with me, girl. You won't need to mingle with them.'

'Ah, but I do need to at least say hello. Come on, back me up, and let's get this over with,' Tory pleaded, leading Carolyn towards Gail and Gordon.

* * *

'See, that wasn't so bad,' Carolyn said with a wry grin and nudged Tory with her elbow as they walked to the bar for a wine refill.

'Did you miss the *"nice to see you, Tory, hope you don't keep Laura out too late, we can take her if you need"* directed at me? Like I'm irresponsible for bringing her here tonight. Not that it might be Brent's decision, too.'

'Chill, sister, you can choose your friends, but you can't choose family.'

'You got that spot on.'

* * *

Saturday dawned. Tory woke with a start as Laura jumped onto Brent as they lay in bed.

180

'Oof,' Brent grunted.

'Wake up, wake up. You promised to take me to ride in the park today,' she said.

'Oh God, not this early,' Brent moaned as he rolled out of bed. 'Breakfast first, munchkin.'

Tory followed, bleary from the late night. The party had been fun. Unlike Laura, who slept across a row of chairs for most of the evening, Tory and Brent didn't get to sleep till late.

The joy of having a young child, she thought as she pulled on her shorts and Tshirt.

At every opportunity, Laura rode the bike she received for Christmas. After wearing a track around the yard, Brent promised to take her to the nearby park, which featured a bike track with its own traffic lights and road. Laura had nagged Brent for weeks to be allowed to ride on the road. Brent compromised by offering to teach her the road rules on the park track.

Tory sat to the side, watching Brent as he explained the rules to Laura. When to stop, what side to ride on, and when she should give way. Laura insisted that Brent pretend to be a car so she could enact the rules correctly around him. Tory laughed at Brent as he panted, running up and down the path, pretending to press a horn and use his blinker at corners. Perspiration dripped down his face. As the day heated up, she thought he would be regretting last night's beer. Laura rode around him, concentrating on what she should be doing, smiling every time she got something right. Tory pulled her mobile from her back pocket and filmed the action.

It was a perfect moment for Tory, and her heart burst with love watching the joy on their faces. As she slid the phone back into her pocket, something made her turn around. She looked up, and at the far end of the park, between two trees, less than a hundred metres away, stood Anton, both hands leaning on his walking stick. He stared at her and lifted his hand, giving a wave and, Tory thought, a smile or perhaps a smirk. The hair on the back of her neck stood up, and adrenaline shot through her body.

'Brent, it's him,' Tory screamed, turning towards Brent.

'What, where?' Brent said as he looked up.

Tory raised her arm, pointing in the direction where Anton had stood moments before. Now, there was just empty space.

'Oh, Brent, he was there, watching us. He smiled, and the creep waved at me.'

Brent ran to where Tory pointed and frantically looked up and down the park and the street. There was no one to be seen. The road was quiet, front yards empty. A few cars were parked on the roadside, but not the white Mercedes Anton drove. Brent looked for a few more minutes. There was no one about.

Brent ran back to Tory, who had her hands on her knees, bent over, hyperventilating. With concern on her face, Laura patted her mother on the back.

'It's okay, Mummy. There is no one there.'

Tory looked at Brent, then her daughter, and threw up.

CHAPTER 32

Tory peered over the steering wheel of Brent's truck at the white Mercedes driving in front of her. Brent left the truck parked in the middle of their driveway and, rather than juggling cars to go to the supermarket, she jumped into the truck. Close to the supermarket, she noticed the Mercedes. It turned right into a side street, and while it was a fair way in front of her, Tory was convinced she saw an elderly, balding man in the driver's seat. Instinctively, she flicked on the blinker and turned the corner to follow him. As she turned the steering wheel, Tory wondered what the hell she was doing. She certainly didn't want to stop him for a chat.

Being in Brent's truck, she hoped he wouldn't twig it was her behind him. Tory followed the Mercedes with caution, keeping as close as she dared. It was an opportune chance, she rationalised, to see where Anton was staying. While she was inexperienced at following someone's car, she felt sure Anton hadn't noticed her. He was driving slowly, like an old guy.

She still thought of Anton as the younger version she had first encountered, and the sight of this old guy felt at odds with her fear of him.

He slowly drove off at the lights and rounded a bend at a snail's pace, causing the car behind him to blare its horn. Several times, she found herself getting too close and so pulled over to allow Anton to gain distance between them. He drove to the town centre. Then, Tory watched his car turn into Aloma's newest motel, the Grandview. Tory pulled into a roadside parking space. She watched him edge his car towards the e-charging outlets. Anton stopped the car, got out, and shuffled down the side of the car to plug in the electric cable. Without looking around, Anton reached in and pulled a walking stick from the car. Tory saw the lights flash as the car locked, and he slowly walked into the front foyer of the motel.

We now know where he is staying. I can't wait to let Brent and Carolyn know, thought Tory, pleased with herself, as she drove back to the supermarket.

* * *

Tory woke feeling lousy again. She must be coming down with something. This week, she struggled to get out of bed each morning, and yesterday, after sighting Anton in the park, she'd vomited. Come to think of it, she wanted to vomit now.

Oh damn, it couldn't be. Realisation hit Tory.

Pregnant? Surely not, not right now.

The idea of being pregnant scared her. Brent wanted more children and would be excited. While Tory wanted more children, she was apprehensive. She loved Laura with every fibre of her body, and it was hard for Tory to imagine having room in her to love another child the same. Her mother hadn't loved her, and she was certain she didn't want to have a child she loved any less than Laura.

Tory sat in a toilet cubicle at work and looked at the blue stripes on the pregnancy test kit she'd picked up at the chemist that morning. Her head spun. This was really happening. The timing was terrible, with Anton hassling them, and she hoped that wouldn't diminish Brent's excitement. Momentarily, she wondered if her head might explode, with so many things to worry about.

Tory sighed and wrapped the test strip in toilet paper and slid it into her handbag. With only a few women working at the office, and her and Carolyn being the only two of childbearing age, she didn't want anyone finding the discarded positive test and spreading rumours before she was ready to tell Frank.

* * *

Brent and Carolyn were sitting outside on the patio in the warmth, catching the last of the afternoon's sunrays, chatting quietly, as Tory walked out from the house toward them. Carolyn followed Tory home again this evening to make sure she had company and stayed safe until Brent arrived. Tory waited until both were there to give them the news together. Anything she told Brent, she told Caro, so they may as well hear it at the same time.

'Guys, I have some news,' she said, looking at them both.

Carolyn clapped her hands to her face.

'OMG, are you …'

Tory nodded, and Carolyn leapt out of her chair and did a dance on the spot.

'Are you what?' asked Brent, looking at them both, puzzled. Then disbelief crossed his face as it dawned on him.

'You're pregnant?'

'Yes, darling,' Tory said, her smile wide.

'Oh, wow.' Brent looked stunned for a moment and then broke into a huge grin.

'That's fantastic,' he said as he lifted her in his arms and swung her around.

'I know the timing is off. I'm not sure how it happened. We must have slipped up on birth control somewhere along the line.'

'It doesn't matter, Tors. This is great news. I am so excited. Laura will love it, too.'

'It's early days. Let's hold off telling anyone else, including Laura, until I am a bit further along.'

'Sounds sensible,' Brent nodded, still grinning.

'Oh, girlfriend, I am so happy for you,' Carolyn said. She, too, wore a broad smile.

They were silent for a moment, each taking in the good news, before another realisation hit the trio. While Anton was around, Tory and the unborn baby were at risk. Brent spoke first, his face serious.

'We need to keep you safe. We can't rely on Caro or me being your bodyguard all the time. We need to end this. To stop the crap that's going on. We need to do something. I'm going to confront Anton and tell him to piss off back to where he came from.'

'Brent, my worry is he won't leave. Just do whatever he planned to do, whatever that might be. If you confront him, someone will see you do it. Then you'll be in trouble,' Tory said. She didn't trust Anton and was worried about Brent.

'You said he got away with pushing your friend's car over the cliff and killing him. Maybe I can do that to him?'

'You think we need to kill him?' Tory asked, shocked, her voice small.

'What do you think, Tory?' Brent replied. He looked at her. 'Do you think he will just go away if we ask him? He's wanted to hurt you for seven years. We have to end it. We can't run forever, or even for ten years. Laura is five years old. She can't be running with us. She needs school and stability. We can't live life looking over our shoulders all the time. Being afraid one of us, you or our child, may be hurt. It's scary. I'm petrified. We can't live like this. We need him gone. Jail or dead. I don't know how to get him in jail. There is no way of proving he killed your friend. We have no way to put him away … not until he kills one of us. I can't think about what that means. We have to get in first.'

Tory and Carolyn looked at each other, their eyes locking. Then, Tory turned to Brent.

'Brent, neither of us are killers. It makes me shudder at the thought. I hesitate when I kill spiders. You're always so kind. You can't be serious?' Tory asked.

'Babe, I am scared for you, for Laura and the baby. I can't think of any other way. He won't just leave if we ask him. He made his intentions abundantly clear when he taunted you. After he went to the centre for Laura, I nearly got in the car to find and kill him then. The police aren't likely to lock him up. So, you will always be at risk while he is alive.'

Tory feared Brent was right, and she knew he meant what he said. Years ago, when she fell pregnant with Laura, she caught her first glimpse of how protective Brent could be toward her. A guy who used to play footy with Brent laughed when he heard she was pregnant and told Brent.

'She's trapped you big time, mate. She's just after your money, I reckon.'

Brent didn't hesitate. His right arm swung around, and his fist smashed into the guy's face.

'Apologise now, you asshole.'

His second punch caused blood to gush from the guy's nose and put him on the ground.

'I said *apologise*,' Brent growled at the guy as he lay on his side.

It took three of his mates to pull Brent away from the bleeding footballer. No one was in any doubt about his feelings for Tory.

'Brent, we don't know the first thing about killing a person. We don't have the right connections to take a contract out on him. If we tried, we would probably end up employing an undercover cop and go to jail ourselves. I can't live with you in jail, and they'd take Laura off us. That's not something I can bear to think about,' Tory said. 'I'm afraid. Will it turn us into something we aren't, or something we don't like? Will we fear each other, knowing what the other is capable of?'

'I would kill to save you and Laura. You heard that here and now. That is the sort of person I am,' Brent replied stubbornly.

'I would kill to save you and her, too. Without a choice, I would do it, too.'

'So that's the sort of people we are. The sort that would do anything to protect each other,' finished Brent, tension filling the air.

'I would kill to keep you safe, too,' Carolyn whispered, her face creased with worry.

Tory jumped. She'd momentarily forgotten Caro. What would she think of this?

* * *

Yesterday, and again today, Carolyn listened to Tory's story of being pursued. The story of Anton at the childcare centre made her angry and fearful for her friends. Tory's family unit meant the world to her. They were her family, too. She wouldn't be here if it weren't for the support and care Tory showed her all those years ago. There was nothing she wouldn't do to help them. Anton crossed the line big time when he attacked her friend.

She also agreed that the police probably couldn't keep them safe. It was a complex situation. If they went to the police to report Anton, and then he was hurt or killed, they would be the first people investigated. There was less chance of the police linking them to his injury or death if there was no obvious connection to Anton in the first place. It was a shame there was no evidence of him killing Tory's friend.

'I love you both. There is no way I could sit by and let that old bastard hurt any of you, especially Laura. That stunt at childcare almost killed me. I want to strangle him with my bare hands,' Carolyn said, her face flushed red with agitation.

'Caro, don't you dare consider it. I don't want to be responsible for getting you in trouble. No way.'

'Well, I'm helping. How are we going to do it?' Carolyn asked.

Tory and Brent looked at each other. It was clear Carolyn meant it.

'I have no idea,' Brent said, desperate to come up with anything.

Tory looked at them both and slowly nodded. 'You are right. He hates me so much. He is never going to go away without hurting me. We can't keep running. Maybe the car over the cliff option is the best way to—'

'You're not thinking rationally,' Carolyn interrupted. 'Forget that idea. There aren't many cliffs around here, and his luxury car probably has auto brakes, sensors, and electronics to tell the police every move it made. You would be caught for sure.'

'Caro, to protect Laura and the unborn baby, Anton needs to die. Do you agree?' Brent asked. He cautiously looked her in the eye.

'Yes, I do. I'm in. But it won't help Tory or the kids if you are caught and put in jail. They need you here, too,' Carolyn said.

'This doesn't seem real. How can we be discussing this?' Tory choked. She shook her head in disbelief.

'I can't see any other way. Unless he drops dead of old age in the next day or so, we have to do something, or he will hurt you, Tory. He has been in town for a week already. He won't plan to stay forever. In fact, my bet is he is planning on doing something soon,' Carolyn said, her face serious.

* * *

Despite what he told Tory, considering killing someone unnerved Brent. An old bloke like Anton could probably have his head bashed in pretty easily, although in the cold light of day, Brent didn't think he could bring himself to do something with so much violence. He didn't have a gun, and he certainly couldn't imagine using a knife to stab anyone, unless he was being attacked himself. He was distressed the few times he hit wildlife in the car. He couldn't imagine what violently ending the life of a person might look like. It didn't sit well on his conscience. Tory was right, too, when she said he shouldn't get caught and go to jail. He didn't want his children raised without a father. They needed to make it look like an accident. Brent didn't know what they were going to do.

'Is there some non-violent way we can kill him?' Tory asked. 'I don't think I could hurt him, if that makes any sense.'

'It makes sense, Tors. I'm thinking the same thing,' Brent said.

Interrupting them, Carolyn stood and picked up her handbag and car keys.

'Okay, let's take some time overnight to think about how we can do it. Whatever you do, don't be a dumbass and search *"how to kill people"* on your phone or computer, or the police will be right onto you when he is killed. Time is running out. We need to come up with something soon. I'll come around tomorrow night. We can work out a plan then.'

Brent nodded as she left.

CHAPTER 33

Anton was getting antsy sitting in his motel suite. He grunted dismissively when he looked around the room. While the suite was fine as far as motel rooms went, he didn't appreciate the replica prints on the wall, listening to the bar fridge hum at night, and sitting on the fabric couch. He missed his leather Chesterfield and the original art hanging on his walls at home, and he resented having to go onto the balcony to avoid the smoke detectors when he lit up a cigar. Seven days in this Hicksville town was far too long.

It was time to kill Tory and go home. He cursed himself for leaving the ammo for his pistol at home. Bloody idiot. When he pulled the Glock from his bag and realised the loaded magazine clip was still at home in his bedside table, his profanity would've made his son in prison blush.

The quickest and easiest way to kill her would have been to use the gun. He smiled to himself, recalling the distress on her face when she'd spotted him at the park. Thank goodness he had the foresight to hire the Toyota Prado for a few days. At the park, when Brent came looking for him, he needed to move quickly, at least quickly for him, to jump in the back of the four-wheel drive and duck down behind the seat. The Prado would provide some anonymity over the next few days while he kept an eye on Tory and checked out the town.

Of course, in Hicksville, renting the Prado was not straightforward.

'I am sorry, sir,' the attendant at the rental company told him. 'We don't usually rent vehicles to someone your age.'

Anton almost exploded with rage.

'I have a perfect driving record and have never been in an accident. Of course, you can rent me a car,' Anton said, his mouth pursed into a snarl, his face turning red.

After significant threats from Anton, and an offer to pay higher insurance and a larger excess, the attendant reluctantly agreed to rent the vehicle. The attendant probably needed stress leave after their interaction.

Anton wondered about using the Prado to finish off Tory.

The rental company could shove it where it fits.

If he drove the rental car at speed into the driver's side of that stupid orange thing she was driving, the Prado would crush the little vehicle and the bitch inside it. He considered playing the old man trick, pleading a medical episode. The trouble with that tactic at his age, he realised, was they might damn well take his driver's licence off him, and he didn't want to take that risk. Another solution may have presented itself, however.

Yesterday, on a drive around town, in an industrial area, Anton fortuitously turned a corner, and the gated property of a motor-cycle club loomed in front of him. A high metal fence with barbed wire looping across the top ringed the property. It looked dark and foreboding. The black sliding gates at the front stood closed. A small sign framed in the fence above the mailbox named the club. Anton was wealthy. He could afford to pay people whatever they wanted to do the job. These guys might be interested. There was no movement at the property as he slowly drove past.

His son would have contacts with this gang. It would only take him a single call to get a name and a number. Trouble is, he knew, any call to his son was likely to be monitored, and he didn't want to take the time to drive all the way to the other end of the state to pay him a visit. Later tonight, he would drive back to the clubhouse in the Prado to look for someone willing to talk.

* * *

Laura was in her room playing, and Tory and Carolyn sat at the kitchen bench, discussing their day. They looked up as Brent walked in carrying a large bunch of flowers.

'For my beautiful, pregnant wife,' he said, bending to kiss Tory as he handed her the flowers.

'Oh, they are gorgeous. Thanks, babe,' Tory said, her face lit up. The rich smell of the lilies filled the air.

'That's it!' Carolyn yelled as she jumped in the air. 'That's how we'll do it!'

Tory and Brent looked at her, startled.

'Do what?' Tory asked.

'Get rid of the creep.'

'Shhh, don't let Laura hear you,' Tory whispered, the smile on her face fading. She put her hand out to calm Carolyn.

'What are you thinking?' Bent asked, curious.

'We'll poison him,' Carolyn said. Her voice was now hushed but firm.

'That's not a solution,' Brent said, shaking his head. 'The cops will test him, and then they'll charge us with murder.'

'Not if it looks like an elderly man having a heart attack,' Carolyn said as she gave them a wicked smile.

'Do tell,' said Tory. She leaned forward toward Carolyn. 'What have you got in mind?'

'There's a plant in my yard which is poisonous and can cause a heart attack. I can extract the poison in the still, and we can slip it into his food.'

Brent was disbelieving. 'No plant grown in someone's backyard can kill a person, surely?'

'There is. In fact, there are many poisonous plants, but we only need the one … and I grow that plant.'

Carolyn explained the story of the seeds her nan planted years ago along the back fence. She grew more and more enthusiastic as she explained to them that the plant was commonly called foxglove. *Digitalis lanata* was its proper name. Drug companies used this plant to make the heart drug digoxin. The whole plant, especially the leaves, was toxic.

'I always wear gloves when I prune them or do any weeding near it, and I never pick the flowers to put in a vase. Have you noticed the pretty, tall-stemmed plant with white-and-yellow flowers that look like little bells? They're behind the roses in the back. The flowers have mostly died off now. This time of year, the plant's mostly only stalks and leaves. It looked really pretty at the start of summer. Nan knew they were poisonous, so she planted the roses in front of it to stop anyone accidentally walking into it.'

'What on earth was your nan thinking?' Brent asked.

Carolyn shrugged.

'Someone gave her the seeds. They were pretty, so we kept them going. We're always careful around the plants. As I said, I always wear gloves and a mask so I don't inhale any particles it might release.'

Brent shook his head in disbelief. 'You never know sometimes, do you?'

'I can pick the leaves and stems and extract the oils in my still. We just need to work out a way to give it to him,' Carolyn said.

'Will it really cause him to have a heart attack?' Brent queried.

'If we give him a high enough dose, it should do. Over the years, there have been lots of stories and warnings on the internet for those of us who make essential oils. There are stories of people getting sick and dying from contact with the plant or inhaling particles from it. There is a whole page devoted to safe handling of the plant.'

'How much will we need?' Tory asked.

Carolyn paused, thinking.

'I don't actually know, but I'll extract as much as I can, and we can give him the lot. Hopefully, that will do it.'

Tory could sense Carolyn's excitement and nodded.

'Well, that's the best idea we have at the moment. When can you do the extraction or whatever it is you need to do?' Brent asked.

'In a few days. I just need to buy more ethanol and pick the plants. It will take a while in the still, so I'll need to do it on the weekend, I guess.'

Hopefully, that will be soon enough, Tory thought, conscious time was against them.

As they watched a smiling Carolyn leave to go home, Brent and Tory looked at each other with a combination of fear and hope. Might this actually work?

Brent whispered in Tory's ear, 'Is it just a little bit scary how enthusiastic Caro seems about this plan?'

CHAPTER 34

Tory stood in front of Carolyn's house admiring the white roses lining the curved path leading to the hot-pink front door. The white-painted, timber house offset the purple of the climbing wisteria draped along the verandah. It was an extremely pretty home. She tapped on the front door. Frank told the office staff earlier today that Carolyn had called in sick. She hadn't responded to any of Tory's text messages, so in her lunch break, Tory came to check she was alright.

'Hi, girlfriend,' Carolyn said. She opened the door and gave Tory a kiss on the cheek.

'Are you okay?' Tory asked as she followed Carolyn into the house.

'Yes, fine. I had too much to do today to go to work,' Carolyn said. She sounded cheery.

'Uh-huh,' Tory said, giving her a questioning look. 'Such as?'

'Well, I decided to do a reconnaissance first thing this morning. I had breakfast with Anton.'

'What! You did what?' Tory spluttered.

As Tory got her breath back, Carolyn told her she spent the morning checking out Anton at the motel.

'It's not like you can do it. I needed more information to work out how and when I can deliver the poison.'

'We didn't say you should make *and* deliver the poison, but tell me, for goodness' sake, what happened?'

Carolyn smiled at her impatience.

'I arrived at the motel early, around seven o'clock, and sat at a table in the café where they serve breakfast. I pretended to read the paper while I checked him out. I sat at a table at the back and got a good view of the room. It turned out to be a very long breakfast. I waited ages for him to show. Eventually, at eight o'clock, he arrived. He shuffled in, leaning on his walking stick. The waitstaff buzzed around him as if he was royalty. They seemed excited when he arrived, certainly more excited than they were when I arrived.

'I got chatting with one of the waitstaff, a lady called Rose. She told me they could set their watch by him. He always comes in at eight, always sits at the same table and eats the same breakfast. They served him a plate of fried eggs and bacon and two coffees,' Carolyn said.

'What if he noticed you watching him?'

'It doesn't matter if he did. I was just pretending to be one of the guests. He doesn't know any different. I ate an awful lot of food this morning, and I'm still buzzing from the three coffees I drank, just to keep the table.'

* * *

Anton was halfway through his breakfast when something made him look up. Across the room, he saw a woman he was sure had been looking at him quickly turn away and stare at the coffee cup in her hands. He admired an attractive woman, and this was one very attractive lady. Her long blonde hair and alabaster oval face shone. Although sitting, at a glance, instinct told him she cut a shapely figure.

Nice-looking broad, he thought as he glanced back to his newspaper and focused on the story in front of him.

* * *

'I can't believe you did that,' Tory said, shaking her head in disbelief. 'At least we have a location to target him now, I suppose.'

'Yes, and I'm going to do it again tomorrow just to make sure he does nothing different on the weekend.'

'Okay. But, Caro, please, be careful.'

'I will. You know me.'

'Unbelievable.' Tory was still in shock and amazed at her friend.

'Come into the garage. I have something to show you,' Carolyn said as she led Tory outside.

Tory followed Carolyn to the garage attached to the side of the house. There were two entrances to the garage. One by the roller door at the front and the other by the small door at the back, through which they now walked. A shoulder-height window in the centre of the back wall provided daylight into the garage.

Tory glanced at the still, set up on a small table at the back. The glassware looked impressive. A large conical flask sat on a stand with a small burner underneath connected to a gas bottle sitting under the table. Carolyn picked up a set of white plastic overalls and held them up to Tory.

'This is the protective suit I'll use to protect myself from any fumes emitted from the plant material. I have a mask, goggles, and gloves too.'

'Where on earth did you get them?' Tory asked in amazement.

'They're easy to find. They're available at any pesticide spray place. I just pretended I was spraying my garden.'

'You're going to look like you came from outer space in that get-up,' Tory giggled.

'I'll start tomorrow as soon as I get back from breakfast at the motel.'

'Thank you, Caro. Are you sure you really want to do this? I mean, it's a pretty horrendous thing we are planning. You will be implicated in murder if something goes wrong and we get caught.'

'Girlfriend, I would do anything to keep you and Laura safe. You're not just a best friend. You're like a sister to me. My life wouldn't be worth living if anything happened to you or to Laura. This guy has crossed the line, and you're in danger. Something needs to happen, and quickly. I want to protect you.'

'That means so much to me. You're like a sister to me, too. I love you. Please be careful, won't you?'

'Careful is my middle name,' Carolyn said, holding out the protective suit.

* * *

Leaving Carolyn's, Tory drove home via the local supermarket. She needed a few things for the weekend. She pulled into the car park and grabbed the shopping bags from the back seat. As she shut the car door, she noticed Detective Blunt walking towards her.

Oh my God, she knows. How could she be aware of the poison plan already? Tory began to panic. They hadn't even got started, and now the police were onto them. Had they bugged her house? she wondered. Was she about to get arrested? What would Brent and Laura do if she was in jail? Would they arrest Brent, too? What would happen to Laura and Carolyn?

'Hello, Tory. Are you alright?' the detective asked.

Tory realised she must have guilt written all over her face. Perspiration beaded her forehead and dripped down, gathering under her jawline.

'Er, yes. Sorry, I was distracted. My mind was in another place,' Tory muttered as she attempted to rearrange her features to reflect calmness. The back of her hand discreetly wiped her face.

'Right, all good then. Have a nice evening,' Detective Blunt said, looking at her oddly before walking off towards the supermarket.

Tory, her heart thumping, got back into her car and sat clasping her hands tightly together to stop them from shaking. She let out one long, relieved breath as her eyes followed Detective Blunt walking away.

CHAPTER 35

Gail drove to Aloma, excited to pick Laura up from school. She'd been looking forward to it all day. With Brent and Tory working, she volunteered to pick up her granddaughter and take her home today, so she didn't have to go to after-school care. Gail offered to get dinner started for the family to give them an easy Friday night. If she didn't, she suspected, Tory would feed them takeaway or some microwavable meal. Bags of groceries sat on the back seat. She was determined they would have a nutritious meal at least one day this week. Brent worked so hard, and with footy training, he needed quality food.

She loved Laura so much and wished she could mind her more often. Tory was so prickly around her. Thankfully, necessity had driven Tory occasionally to ask her to mind Laura. Brent gave her a house key, which made things easier, but she understood she needed to be careful how often she used it. Gail didn't want Tory demanding the key back.

On the way back from school, Laura chatted nonstop, filling Gail in on all the dramas in the school grounds. As Gail steered the car into their driveway, Laura spoke.

'Oh, good. That bad man in the white car isn't here.'

'What do you mean, *bad man*, Laura?' Gail asked. Her voice was tinged with caution, and her heart gave a quick flutter.

'There is a bad man after mummy. I heard them talking. They don't know I know. He tried to pick me up from the centre last week, too, but wasn't allowed. Mummy and Daddy have been fighting, but they told me they are not getting a divorce.'

Laura's words shocked Gail. She looked into the rear-vision mirror and saw Laura looked happy enough. She was aware of an increase in tension between Tory and Brent since Tory's purse and car were stolen and her previous identity came to light. Perhaps things were worse than she realised. As much as Tory annoyed Gail by the way she controlled her son and granddaughter, and while she suspected Tory's name change meant she did undesirable things as a younger person, someone trying to harm her daughter-in-law and granddaughter was another thing entirely. Laura's story of someone trying to pick her up from the centre tied in with the odd call Gordon received from Brent earlier. It now started to make sense.

Gail would not stand by and watch someone hurt her family. Not a chance. After settling Laura down to do her homework while munching on some afternoon tea, Gail pulled out her mobile phone and called her husband. She spoke quietly to Gordon, and together they made a plan. As Gail spoke, she looked at Laura to make sure the young girl with bionic hearing was not listening to their conversation. She ended the call and waited for Gordon to arrive.

* * *

Tory turned the orange car onto their street and looked toward her house to see both Gail's and Gordon's cars parked out the front.

What on earth?

She pulled into the garage just as Brent drove up behind her. She felt relieved not to have to face them on her own.

'Hi, Tors. What's Dad doing here?' Brent asked, coming around to her side of the car.

'Your guess is as good as mine.' Tory shrugged as they walked through the front door.

Gail and Gordon sat with Laura at the kitchen table. Laura seemed to be mid-story when they turned to look as Brent and Tory entered.

'Hey, Mum, Dad. What's happening?' Brent greeted them.

'Laura, darling, can you please run outside and play on the swing for a bit? We want to talk to your mum and dad,' Gail asked.

'So you can talk grown-up stuff, I bet,' Laura said, rolling her eyes as she walked out the door to the backyard.

Brent looked at his mother. 'What's happened?'

'Why didn't you tell us someone was after Tory? Don't you think we can help you?'

Tory stepped forward, looking from Gail to Gordon and back. 'Who told you that?'

'Your daughter. She hears more than you realise,' Gail replied, looking at Laura through the glass doors as she played on the swing set.

'You should have told us, Brent,' Gordon said sternly.

'Dad, we aren't sure what to do. We're in the middle of trying to figure that out at the moment.'

'So, it's true, then. Is Laura safe? Have you gone to the police?' Gail bristled.

Brent shrugged his shoulders. 'We're being careful. Tory always has someone with her, so she isn't alone. We don't have any strong proof to take to the police, so we're wanting to try something else first.'

'If you don't have proof, then what's been the trigger?'

Brent explained to them the notes left in the mailbox and how they'd seen Anton at the park.

'He tried to pick Laura up, the day I called and asked if Dad went to the centre.'

'He better not harm Laura or Tory,' Gail shouted, her voice raised and her eyes narrowing.

Tory couldn't believe the change in Gail. Whatever Laura said to her grandmother earlier today seemed to flick a switch. This evening, Gail and Gordon's priority was protecting Tory and Laura. Gail became the protective lioness. For the first time, Tory felt included, part of Brent's family. They had her back. It was odd, but comforting.

Gordon asked what the 'something else' was that Brent wanted to try first. There was no way either Tory or Brent would tell them about the poison. Brent looked at Tory and spoke vaguely, leading his parents to believe they planned to confront Anton, to sort things out. Tory's mouth gaped, gobsmacked when Brent's father offered to be muscle for him.

'If you need back up, Son, say the word. I'll be there in a heart-beat,' Gordon volunteered.

Gail and Gordon offered to take Laura to stay with them for a few days.

'Just to keep her safe and make sure the guy doesn't frighten her.'

Relieved, Tory agreed. The next few days and nights could see things come to a head, and she didn't want Laura caught in the crossfire. An excited Laura rushed off to pack when they told her.

Tory and Brent stood in the doorway waving as they drove off. Laura sat up front in Grandma's car. Brent took Tory's hand in his own and gave it a squeeze.

'I'll be damned. I've never seen those two so riled. It looked like they would slay dragons for you. How about Dad offering to back me up in a fight,' Brent said in awe.

Tory shook her head, amazed. 'It felt nice. It's a shame it's taken this to show me they care.'

'They've always cared,' Brent said. 'Mum just had a funny way of showing it, I guess.'

'Well, now we have the evening to ourselves, with no eaves-dropper, let me tell you what Caro did today.'

CHAPTER 36

When Tory left, Carolyn kept going over and over in her mind the things she needed to do. The anticipation thrilled her, but with so many things on her list, she worried she might run out of time.

She looked at her watch. It was three in the afternoon. Still plenty of time left in the day to start a batch. She may as well start now.

Carolyn headed into the backyard and opened the garage's side door. She walked in and flicked on the switch to the single-bulb light hanging from a roof beam. The bulb emitted a dull light, but with the few hours of sunlight left, the natural light coming in the back window would brighten the space. Since Tory now had Nan's car, the garage was mostly empty. Gardening tools leaned against a wall. The only other items were a fold-out chair, which she used to sit and watch over the still while it worked, and the still itself, sitting on a small table.

A hose ran from a bucket filled with water to the still. The hose connected to a small pump plugged into a power board. A small gas burner sat under the Pyrex conical flask. She remembered when the still arrived in the mail years ago. It was an exciting time. After a few mishaps, Carolyn correctly connected the various parts and set it into action. The first few batches did not work out. Now, however, after much practice, Carolyn extracted quality oils. The oils made good money at the local markets, although, she reflected, if she converted the time it took to distil the oils into an hourly rate, she probably should charge much more for her products. Today, it didn't matter how long it took. This distillation had a more important purpose.

Carolyn picked the coveralls off the table and put them on over her clothes. She pulled the filtered face mask down over her nose and mouth and, lastly, pulled on long rubber gloves. She picked up a large, black, plastic garbage bag and her secateurs and went outside to the garden.

Carolyn needed to take extra care when she stepped up to the foxglove plants. The roses Nan planted in front were a good deterrent for anyone walking too close to the foxglove. However, the roses might prove problematic if she tore her protective suit on a thorn. She carefully edged her way around the roses. Her hands pressed the suit towards her body, away from the thorns.

Carolyn leant over the foxglove flowers and snipped them at their base. There were six tall plants. With one hand holding the garbage bag open, she gently lifted the plants one by one and slipped them inside, closing the top shut with her left hand. She thought six plants should be plenty for distilling. In fact, it would take several sessions in the still to use all six. Carolyn knew she only had one shot at this. She'd picked all the foxglove.

As she walked back to the garage, Carolyn heard a knock at her front door.

Damn it. She had no time for visitors. Dressed in her protective gear, gripping the bag of poisonous plants, she slipped into the garage and shut the door.

'Caro, are you there?' a voice called from the front porch.

It was Karl. What was he doing here? He should be at work.

Carolyn held her breath. He probably called around to check on her after she called in sick. She crossed her fingers he wouldn't walk around to the backyard looking for her. She stood, frozen, waiting to see what he would do next. *Curses!* Her car was parked in the driveway. He would know she was home.

The minutes dragged on, then she heard a car door close and the car drive away. Carolyn breathed out with relief. That was too close. A message beeped on her mobile phone. She wriggled off the glove on her free hand and picked up the phone, which sat next to the still. It was a text from Karl telling her he'd called around to check how she was and guessed she must be sleeping.

Yes, that's it. I was sleeping. I will message him back later when I 'wake up', she thought with a smile.

Carolyn slipped the glove back on and carefully reached into the bag to pull the leaves and a few remaining flowers from the stalks. For the best yield, Carolyn normally dried the plants before she extracted the oils. On this occasion, however, there wasn't enough time. The plant was starting to dry, anyway. The plants had finished blooming a few weeks ago, and with the late heat of summer, many of the tiny bell flowers were dry or had fallen off.

Whatever oil I get will have to do, she thought as she placed the flowers and leaves into the conical flask sitting at the top of the still.

After filling the flask with the foliage, she connected all the tubing and turned the hotplate on to heat the water solvent in the base flask. From there, it would send steam up through the flask and the plant material and then carry the oils up to the condenser and, ultimately, the separator, where she would collect the poison. She would add an aqueous ethanol to enhance the solvent process a bit later.

Carolyn picked up her phone and moved her chair a safe distance away from any fumes, to the far end of the garage. She'd downloaded a novel on her phone to read while she monitored the distillation process. Wearing the protective gear for the two or so hours the process took would be uncomfortable, and the novel would help pass the time.

*　*　*

Carolyn looked at the time on her phone. Two and a half hours should be enough. She stood up, stretched, and walked rigidly to the still. Her muscles felt stiff from sitting so long, and perspiration soaked her clothes. The plastic overalls, combined with the warmth of the late-summer day, had caused her to sweat profusely. She turned off the hotplate and checked the separator. A line of oil floated above the water in the collection flask. She drained off the water and picked up a small glass ampule. She held it under the release valve and turned the tap. Two to three millilitres of oil slid into the ampule. Carolyn held it up to the light. The clear, oily liquid glistened.

It looked good.

She carefully placed the ampule to one side and started the cleaning process for the still. Not trusting the safety of the used flowers and leaves, she carefully placed them into a fresh plastic bag and sealed the top. She would bury it later.

Carolyn peeled off her gloves and walked back into the house, where she pulled off the face mask and climbed out of the overalls, setting them on her kitchen bench. She could smell herself. She desperately needed a wash.

As she stepped out of the shower, she heard a knock at the door. She quickly dried herself and threw on a fresh T-shirt and shorts.

'Caro, are you there?' Karl called out.

'Coming!' she called back. As she walked to the front door, she glanced at the protective gear sitting on the bench and winced.

Carolyn opened the door a fraction and poked her head out.

'Hi, Karl. What are you doing here?'

'I came by earlier to check on you. When you didn't answer the door or a text I sent you, I figured I better call in again after work to make sure you hadn't passed out or something.'

Damn, I forgot to send the bloody text.

'Thanks, Karl. I'm good now. Just slept most of the afternoon,' she lied.

'I'm glad you're okay.' Karl stood at the door awkwardly.

The protective suit lying on the kitchen bench taunted Carolyn. She couldn't invite him in. She had to come up with something fast.

'Sorry, I can't ask you in because the place is a mess. Thanks for coming to check on me, though. I'll catch up with you later, okay?'

God, that was lame, she thought.

A look of puzzlement and hurt flicked across Karl's face as Carolyn shut the door. She felt annoyed with herself for putting Karl in this position.

She should've put the suit away before getting in the shower. Carolyn stood with her back to the door until she heard Karl drive away.

Carolyn planned to have a rest, eat some dinner, and then go back to the garage to make a second brew. Unsure if the flower/leaf-combination oil would be strong enough, she wanted to do an extraction from the stalks and remaining leaves. As she sat at the dining table, eating a microwave meal she'd heated a few minutes earlier, her phone pinged with a text message from Tory.

Hey C. what did you do to Karl?

Hey GF. Nothing. He visited when I had the protective gear in the kitchen. I couldn't let him in. Did he say something?

Asked Brent if he was misreading situation, thought you liked him, now not sure

Damn GF, I DO like him. Bad timing. Ask Brent to set him straight plz.

Will do. Don't tell him what you r doing, whatever you do. He will freak

Don't plan on telling

Good. We r having a quiet night. Laura @ grandies

Brewing tonight, C U tomorrow.

Good luck XXX

Carolyn didn't mean to upset Karl, but rescuing Tory from the dangerous old guy was a priority. Karl would just have to wait his turn. Carolyn finished her meal, then picked up the overalls and mask and headed to the garage for another long session.

* * *

The alarm startled Carolyn, and she quickly sat up.

Damn. She was so out of it. It was a good thing she set the alarm, or she might not have woken in time.

Making the second brew last night had been exhausting. Carolyn didn't normally do two lots in one day, nor did she usually need to wear breathing gear and protective clothing. After draining off the second ampule of oil, Carolyn wearily climbed out of her gear, showered for the second time that day, and fell exhausted into bed.

Now she jumped out of bed, quickly dressed in the pink pantsuit she'd laid out the previous night, ran a brush through her long hair, and slipped on a pair of heels. She grabbed the keys to her car and rushed out the door. She needed to get to the motel before eight o'clock to be seated at her table before Anton arrived.

CHAPTER 37

Carolyn walked through the motel doors a few minutes before eight. She picked up a thick Saturday newspaper from the concierge desk, paused, and looked around the restaurant. The restaurant décor was modern, with white walls, funky cane-woven lampshades hanging from the ceiling, lime-washed wooden tables and chairs, and a single orange gerbera in a vase at the centre of each table. A bright blue-and-white patterned cushion sat on each chair, giving the room a beach atmosphere. Anton was not at his table. She puffed out a breath in relief.

A couple sat at the table she chose yesterday, so Carolyn slipped into a seat at the adjacent table. Within minutes, the red-haired Rose, who served her last time, approached and handed her a menu.

'Do you want a coffee while you decide what to order?'

'A skinny latte, please,' Carolyn answered, and Rose tapped her request into an electronic notepad.

The restaurant seemed quieter than yesterday. People, mainly couples, occupied six tables with a further ten tables set ready for guests. Only Anton's table held a reserved placard. Carolyn smelt the delicious aroma of bacon wafting in from the kitchen, causing her stomach to grumble. She opened the first page of the paper. Head down, appearing to read, Carolyn discreetly observed Anton, newspaper under one arm, shuffle in and head straight to his table. Rose raced in with a coffee, smiling at Anton as she placed it in front of him.

Carolyn looked at her watch. Eight o'clock on the dot.

After serving Anton, Rose headed her way.

'Have you decided what you would like to order?'

'Yes, thanks. I'll have bacon and scrambled eggs. Looks like your man was on time today again,' Carolyn said and nodded in the direction of Anton.

Rose looked over at Anton.

'Yes,' she said, sighing. 'It's a shame he won't be here much longer. It's been yonks since someone tipped this well. In fact, I don't think I've ever been tipped so well.'

'Oh. When is he leaving?' Carolyn asked, trying to sound casual.

'Booked out on Wednesday. It was good while it lasted, I guess,' she said, shrugging her shoulders.

As Rose walked off, Carolyn got out her phone and sent a quick text to Tory.

Hey GF. Our man is checking out Wednesday. Talk later.

They were running out of time. She should probably do the deed tomorrow. The thought sent a jolt of electricity through Carolyn. *Wow.* It was thrilling. It was real. She was determined to protect Tory, Laura, and the baby. Suddenly, she felt nervous.

I'll need to time everything perfectly. One shot is all I'll get at this.

I can't afford to fail for Tory's sake, and I don't want to end up in jail.

As she ate her eggs, Carolyn observed Anton. He followed the same routine as yesterday. Coffee, eggs, and a second coffee. She watched him wipe his mouth with a napkin, push his chair back, and stand. The waitress, Rose, rushed over to him, and they spoke briefly. Anton shook his head, clearly annoyed as he walked out. A look of worry crossed Rose's face.

Carolyn stood and walked to the concierge desk to pay for her meal. She paid in cash, just as she had the day before. She wanted to limit any trail that could identify her. To make it harder for police to investigate.

'Thank you, madam,' the young man said as he took her money. 'Just to let you know, we have a function here tomorrow morning. We have an arrangement with a café down the street for guests to get a twenty percent discount off breakfasts on Sunday. If you wish to go there, show them your room key for the discount.'

'Thank you. Will you be open Monday morning?' Carolyn asked.

The concierge nodded. 'Yes, Monday as usual.'

Carolyn walked out towards her car.

Damn. No doubt the function was what made Anton so annoyed. With the restaurant closed, she didn't dare use the poison tomorrow. It wasn't worth the risk of trying the café with an unfamiliar menu and seating arrangements. Anton might not stick to his routine and order a different meal. He might not even go there for breakfast.

No. She'd have to do it on Monday.

* * *

Anton was sick of this shithole town. There was no way he wanted to stay here another week. He'd booked the motel until Wednesday. After that, they wouldn't see him for dust. The bloody motorbike club so far had been a bust. Every day, Anton drove past the club, both during the day and evening, and there was no sign of anyone there.

Where the bloody hell are they?

He'd even walked to their gate and banged on it to find out if someone was inside. A camera set up on the tall gate looked down at him. He waved to the camera, and with his hand, he mimed a phone signal. Then, he held up his phone and typed out his phone number. Nothing. The camera was probably a bloody fake, used as a deterrent. Either that or they weren't monitoring it regularly. Regardless, he grew more and more pissed off each day.

Finally, he decided to implement Plan B. He would do it himself. Take the risk of convincing the police it was an accident. Convince them his foot slipped in the hire car, a car he wasn't overly familiar with. He would tell them, 'Officer, I went for the brake and accidentally pushed full force on the accelerator.'

That should do the trick, he hoped.

While tailing Tory, Anton noticed on Tuesdays she left work half an hour early to pick up her daughter. Between leaving work and driving to the centre, she was alone in the car. Her route took her past several quiet intersections.

I'll get her at one of those. I'll ram the bloody Prado into the side of her car so hard she won't stand a chance.

Meanwhile, he needed to find something to do for the next two days, and somewhere else to eat breakfast tomorrow.

CHAPTER 38

'Hey, Brent, do you reckon we are safe enough to pick up Laura for the weekend?' Tory asked, holding her phone to him so he could see the text from Carolyn.

'Yeah, I reckon. Wednesday, bloody hell. That means he's likely to be planning something on Monday or Tuesday. I'll call Mum and tell her we can take Laura tonight and bring her back tomorrow. She can pick Laura up from care Monday and Tuesday and take her to their home for those nights.'

* * *

Carolyn drove straight from the motel to Brent and Tory's house.

'He followed exactly the same routine as yesterday. He's so arrogant. I can't stand him. He had the waitstaff spinning circles for him, although with the way he apparently tips, she didn't seem to mind.'

'The creep. Just talking about him gives me shivers,' Tory said.

'I finished the poison last night. It's ready to go.'

'Holy hell. I still can't believe this,' Brent muttered. 'When will you do it?'

'I want to wait until Monday. With the booking at the restaurant tomorrow, his morning routine will change, and I don't want to risk mucking it up.'

Tory and Brent looked at each other. It was getting real now. Once they went down this rabbit hole, succeed or fail, there was no going back. In unison, they nodded to Carolyn.

'Thanks, Caro,' Brent said, his voice cracking. 'We're so grateful you're doing this. I can't imagine what else we might've done. You're a lifesaver.'

'Anything to keep you guys safe, always,' Carolyn said as she put her arms around both of them.

Tory and Carolyn left Brent at home to mow the lawn and drove to pick up Laura.

As they pulled into Gail and Gordon's driveway, Laura ran out.

'Mummy!' she said and leapt into Tory's arms.

'Darling.' Tory hugged her, looking behind Laura to Carolyn, who nodded, understanding how precious this little girl was.

'Mummy, Grandma says you are the best mummy, and you work really hard for us.'

Tory stood back and looked at Laura, stunned. This would be the first time she heard Gail say anything nice about her. Tory looked up to Gail standing in her doorway, watching them with a smile. Tory nodded a thanks to Gail, who returned the nod. As she set Laura in the car and secured her seat belt, Tory's mind sped a million miles an hour. Perhaps, just perhaps, she might start to feel part of the family. The past terrible few months, if nothing else, might have led to Gail accepting her. Feelings of gratitude swelled inside her. Her mother never cared for her, but perhaps Gail did now. Tory smiled to herself. It was strangely comforting.

'Well, girlfriend, that's a turn-up for the books,' Carolyn acknowledged, looking at Tory, eyebrows raised.

Tory shrugged with a grin on her face. 'Miracles apparently do happen,' she said, shaking her head in wonder.

On the way back home, Tory drove into the supermarket car park.

'I just need to duck in for a few things. Are you right to stay in the car or do you want to come with me?'

'We'll be good here. That okay with you?' Carolyn asked, turning to Laura.

'Yep. Caro and I can talk,' Laura said, sounding fifteen instead of five years old.

Tory opened the boot and pulled out her shopping bags, then walked toward the store.

As Carolyn and Laura sat talking, Carolyn's phone rang.

Carolyn looked at the caller display. It was Nan.

'Laura, it's Nan. I should take this, okay?'

Laura nodded.

'Hi, Nan. How are you?' Carolyn said as she stepped out of the car.

Carolyn talked to her while keeping an eye on Laura in the car. Laura blissfully played with a doll she had pulled from her overnight bag.

Carolyn filled Nan in on the week's events. Knowing Nan would keep her secrets, she shared everything with her.

'Nan, you won't believe it, that foxglove is going to finally come in handy. We need to stop a man in his tracks, well, actually end it for him. I've brewed the plant, and it's ready to slip to him. Hopefully, the plant superpowers will do the trick.'

'Should've used it on that horrible nurse I had last month,' Nan said, chuckling. 'Glad it's finally going to be useful. You be careful, Carolyn. Don't get any on you.'

'I've been very careful. I nearly got caught by Karl, though. I felt a bit mean. He came around at the wrong time, and I wouldn't talk to him.'

'He'll be alright. Ask him out next week. He'll forget about it.'

'I hope so. I really like him.'

'He's a lucky man,' Nan said.

Carolyn saw Tory, carrying two bags, walk through the glass sliding doors of the supermarket. 'Thanks, Nan. I had better go. Love you.'

'Love you too, darling.'

Tory put the groceries into the boot and slid into the driver's seat.

'All good?' she asked, looking at them both, and they nodded to her. She turned the key, revved the engine, and drove home.

* * *

Later, sitting on the patio with Brent and Tory, Carolyn suddenly exclaimed, 'I've got something to show you.' She reached into her bag and pulled out a small black box.

In front of them, Carolyn opened the box and held it so both could look inside. The small glass ampule sat on a handcrafted stand similar to those she used for her most precious oils when they were to be sold as gifts.

'Is that it?' asked Brent, awe in his voice.

Carolyn nodded. 'This is the more concentrated one. I was

worried the first one might not be strong enough, so I made a second batch using the stalks. Apparently, they contain more of the poison.'

'Will it work?' asked Tory.

'I hope so. I've never done this before, and it's not like I can test it, can I?' Carolyn said.

'Mate, if this works, you've got our gratitude forever,' Brent said.

'Even if it doesn't, you've got it,' responded Tory as she placed her hand on Carolyn's. 'We're stunned you are doing this for us. You can change your mind if you want. We'd understand.'

'Girlfriend, there is no question of doing this for you. We need to make sure you are safe. We love you,' she said, looking at Tory.

'I feel sick. What if something goes wrong? What if he doesn't die, or you get caught?'

'Then we work out what we need to do next. Let's not worry about that until we need to.'

'If she gets caught, I will say it was all my idea, and I bullied her into it,' Brent interrupted.

'Yeah, right,' scoffed Carolyn. 'I am the one with the still. No one will believe it was your idea. Don't worry. I won't get caught, anyway.'

'I hope not. We'd be devastated. You've been so good to us,' Tory said, looking at Carolyn. 'We love you too.'

The three of them chatted for a while longer, then Carolyn left to go home. As she was leaving, she told them, 'I'll call around tomorrow night. You can help me practise getting the stuff into his coffee so I'll be right for Monday morning.'

CHAPTER 39

Sunday arrived, and Tory planned to spend a quiet day at home with Brent and Laura before they drove to Gail and Gordon's to leave Laura for the two-night sleepover.

Tory carried her morning coffee to the patio to join Brent and enjoy the last warmth of summer. She watched Laura, with her serious five-year-old face, walk out the door towards her.

'Hello, darling. Why are you looking so worried? What's up?'

'Mummy, what's a rock dove flower? Caro says it can stop a man in his tracks. I want to give it to Connor to stop him from pulling my pigtails.'

Tory spat out her coffee, coughing as it went down the wrong way. She tried to contain the combination of horror and amusement showing on her face. Horror that Laura had overheard a conversation about the foxglove and its poison, and amusement at the practical way Laura was planning to stop a boy teasing her.

'Sorry, Laura. There is no such thing. Caro must've been joking when she told that story.'

'Oh. Bummer. I'll stomp on his toes, then.'

'I am not sure that is a good idea either,' Tory replied, chuckling.

'Did you ask him to stop?'

'Nah, I just run away. He doesn't chase me too far because I am so fast,' Laura said, puffing her chest out with pride.

'Well, if he does it again, yell at him to stop and see how you go with that.'

'Okay.' With that, Laura ran off back inside.

Tory turned to Brent.

'Shit, she hears everything. I am sure we never spoke about the foxglove in front of her. We've got to be more careful. The thought she might work out what we are doing horrifies me.'

Brent nodded. 'You should tell Caro to be careful as well. She forgets how crafty Laura can be when she wants to know what's going on.'

'Too right. We don't want her knowing what we've been involved in or telling anyone either. It might send us to jail.'

Later that evening, with Laura at her grandparents, Carolyn arrived back at their house. She looked gorgeous as usual, dressed in a short denim skirt and a pink crop top, her hair in a single braid down her back.

Tory gave her a welcoming kiss on the cheek as she walked through the door.

'Evening. You look good.'

'Ta. You too, girlfriend. Nice dress. Munchkin at the grandies?'

Tory nodded. Tory wore a spaghetti-strapped, floral maxi dress that flowed softly around her body as she walked.

'Okay, let's do this,' Carolyn said.

She directed Brent to sit at the table with a coffee cup in front of him.

Together they practised over and over, using a similar-shaped vial to the one that stored the poison. The vial contained olive oil to mimic the viscosity of the poison extract. She practised bumping into Brent, holding his attention for a moment, and at the same time, without looking at her right hand holding the vial, flicking off the lid and upending its contents into the cup. She practised holding the vial discreetly in one hand, opening and tipping so as not to spill any of the oil on herself.

The oil was more viscose than water and poured a fraction slower.

'I'll need to hold the vial over the cup for slightly longer than if it was water,' Carolyn said, concentration lines creasing her forehead.

'You'll need to create some sort of distraction for a second or two,' Brent suggested.

'You're right. Otherwise, I'm worried holding the vial over his coffee and pausing will make it obvious to Anton.'

'I am not sure, Caro. You're emptying the vial pretty well now,' Tory said. 'Maybe if you take the cap off before you approach his table, it might be faster?'

'Yes, I can try that. I'll need to be careful not to spill the oil on myself, though.'

Thirty minutes later and after a dozen practice runs, Brent stood.

'Ouch,' Brent said. He rubbed his shoulder. 'That is enough accidental bumping. I'm getting bruised.'

'I'm pretty confident now,' Carolyn said. 'The accidental bump seems pretty smooth and realistic. What do you guys think?'

'You do it well. It looks real to me,' Tory said. Brent nodded his agreement.

'Okay, we are right for tomorrow, then,' Carolyn said. 'I just hope he doesn't look at his coffee before he drinks it, in case he notices an oily film on the top and gets suspicious.'

'Will he taste it? He might not drink it if it tastes funny,' Tory asked.

'I don't actually know if it tastes like anything. Because it's poison, there is no description of what it tastes like anywhere on the internet. I don't think it matters, though. He downs the macchiato after his breakfast in one swig, so even if it tastes bad, it will be too late; he's swallowed it already,' Carolyn said.

'That's good.' Tory nodded.

'Caro, we need to talk about what to do if you get caught,' Brent said.

'Yes, we should come up with a plan for the worst-case scenario,' Tory said.

'I can't imagine getting caught. If Anton sees me put the oil in his coffee, I'll simply knock the coffee over so there is nothing to sample. If he doesn't drink it, no one will be the wiser. If he drinks it and doesn't die but needs treatment, I assume the medics will assess him for heart problems. Why would they test an old guy for poison?'

'I don't know, Caro, but the idea of spilling his coffee if he sees you slip in the poison is good,' Brent said.

'I'm happy with what's planned. Are you good to go, Tors?' Carolyn asked with a good-natured challenge in her tone.

'I just wish we could fast forward till tomorrow. To when it's all done. I'm so nervous.'

'It will be over soon enough, girlfriend.' And with that, a confident Carolyn left for home.

CHAPTER 40

Tory woke early on Monday. Brent slept peacefully beside her. She'd had trouble sleeping last night. Sitting in bed now, her heart raced, and her chest felt tight. She wasn't sure if the nausea she was feeling was because of the baby or because she was nervous. She slid out of bed, slipped a sundress on over her head, and padded to the kitchen. Tory held her coffee in shaky hands. Sitting at the dining table staring into space, thoughts ran through her overactive mind. What options did she have if today proved unsuccessful? Anton would try to kill her. She could be sure about that. She knew he would try soon, today or tomorrow. It frightened her. She put her hand on her stomach.

'I can't let anything happen to you, little one,' she whispered.

Although she knew it wasn't possible, she wanted to go with Caro to the motel, to support her and watch the event unfold. She wanted to be there when that evil man, the cause of all her problems, died. The process concerned her a little. She didn't want to see him suffer, just to know it was over. Anton had pushed her and Brent into a corner. He'd given them no choice but to act. He would hurt them if they didn't hurt him first.

Tory felt helpless and guilty. Brent was so good to her, and she had kept her past hidden. Not told him her secrets. And in doing so, she'd put Brent, Laura, and their unborn child's lives at risk. Not to mention her wonderful friend Caro. The gratitude Tory felt for Caro was immeasurable. She hoped she could repay her someday.

* * *

Carolyn also woke early. She lay in bed, eyes on the strip of light above the curtains as it grew lighter and brighter with the morning sun rising in the sky. She looked at her bedside clock. The glowing digits showed it was six in the morning.

Two hours to kill.

She giggled at her silliness.

She dressed carefully, selecting a long white pantsuit to enhance her height and set off her summer tan. She added strappy high heels, which helped her to sway sexily as she walked. She wanted to distract Anton, and anyone else, from taking notice of what she held in her hand.

The time had arrived. No changing her mind. One hundred percent commitment.

Today was the day they would get rid of Anton. At least she hoped that's what would happen. She opened the linen-press door where she kept hidden the two vials of foxglove oils. She selected the vial with the most concentrated poison, picked up her handbag, and walked outside. In the driveway, she opened her car door and leant into the passenger side, placing her handbag on the seat and setting the vial gently beside it.

Carolyn drove carefully to the motel. She didn't want to attract the attention of the police. The last thing she needed was a fine or some other evidence placing her near the motel.

Carolyn parked her car against the kerb opposite the motel. The morning felt warm, already on the way to reach the forecasted thirty-three degrees. She looked across to the sliding doors of the motel as they opened. A woman in skimpy exercise gear emerged and began jogging down the street towards the botanic gardens. Carolyn tingled with excitement and nervous energy. She took a deep breath.

Carolyn looked at the time. Seven fifty. Tension coursed through her body.

She got out of the car, walked around to the passenger side, and opened the door. She reached in and pulled out her handbag. As the bag swung out, she watched in horror as it clipped the vial and brushed it off the seat. She heard a gentle clunk as it hit the road and rolled.

'Oh no!' she gasped.

As if in slow motion, too slowly, she bent down to retrieve the vial and watched helplessly as it rolled into the opening of the stormwater drain under the car. The vial landed with a soft tinkle, a long distance from where she stood.

'Oh fuck!' she exclaimed.

'Shit, shit, shit.'

What was she going to do? *Think.* She glanced at her wrist-watch. It was five minutes to eight. Damn it. There was no more time. She had to rush home, get the other vial, and be back before Anton finished his breakfast.

'Please let the vial at home be potent enough,' Carolyn muttered to herself as she ran around to the driver's side, swinging the door open and jumping in. She started the car and flattened her foot on the accelerator, determined to make it back in time.

Back at the motel, she slammed the car into park and pulled the handbrake. Breathless, Carolyn grabbed her handbag from the front seat, which, this time, held the second precious vial. She swiftly walked into the motel. At the restaurant, she took a calming breath and tried to look casual. As she walked to a table at the back, she breathed a sigh of relief when her eyes locked on Anton, who sat at his table, eating the last of his breakfast. She calmed herself, and as she sat down, a member of staff greeted her. To Carolyn's relief, it was a male who approached her. After her questions on Saturday, she worried Rose might get suspicious if she noticed Carolyn was at the restaurant the morning Anton died.

'What would you like today?'

Carolyn suddenly realised she wouldn't have time to eat before Anton left.

'Ah, I have just received a text,' she said with a covering lie. 'I have to leave unexpectedly. Can I just have a coffee to go, a cappuccino, please?'

'Sure. Won't be long. You can collect it at the front counter if you don't mind waiting there.'

'Okay, thanks.' Carolyn handed him five dollars.

As she ordered her coffee, Carolyn watched a waitstaff remove Anton's empty plate from the table and place a small coffee by his right hand. He smiled at her and slipped some folding money into her hand.

It's now or never. Carolyn stood from her seat, and her hand reached into her handbag, fingers closing around the vial. Heart thumping, she made her way quickly towards Anton's table.

* * *

Anton felt a sudden thud as someone collided heavily into his back. Shocked, he turned as blonde hair flicked across his face.

'Oh my God. I am so sorry,' the beautiful blonde said as she braced herself, putting both hands on the table in front of him. 'I must've tripped on something.'

The table jolted as she steadied herself and stood up.

'That's okay, love. No damage done,' he said, reaching out to pat her arm.

'Sorry,' she said again as she pulled her arm away, her face flushed.

'Nothing spilt, fortunately,' he said.

She looked at him and then quickly moved away.

What a funny thing, he thought as his eyes followed the woman he'd seen in the restaurant over the past few days. She picked up a takeaway coffee from the concierge desk and walked out, her long legs sashaying sexily.

Shame I didn't get to know her, he thought with a smirk.

Anton gulped down his macchiato and curled his lips in distaste. It was the worst coffee he'd tasted since he arrived. His mouth felt coated in fur.

I need to clean my teeth, get rid of this taste. I can't wait to get out of this shithole, he thought, thinking of the quality coffee they made at the place around the corner from his home.

Anton walked to the lift to take him back to his room, where he planned to collect his car keys, then follow Tory on her morning drive to work.

One last day of following her. Then tomorrow, I'll do the deed and get the hell out of this dump.

CHAPTER 41

Carolyn hurried to her car and slumped into the driver's seat. She lay her head back on the headrest and tried to catch her breath and calm herself. She'd done it! While Anton patted her left arm, her right hand emptied the vial into his short coffee. No one seemed to notice. She picked up her cappuccino from the concierge desk and glanced back in time to watch Anton throw back his coffee in a single swig, just as she'd hoped. Now, fingers crossed the poison worked.

Carolyn called Tory on her mobile.

'Hey, girlfriend. It's done.'

'Did it work? Is he …' Tory stopped. She didn't want to say something on the phone that might get them into trouble. She wished right now they'd been smart enough to prearrange code words.

'I can't tell. I had to leave as soon as I did it. I'll wait here for a bit to watch if anything happens. I'll catch up with you at work.'

'Thank you, Caro. You're the best.' Tory hung up.

Desperate to find out if the poison worked, Tory got ready for work in a fluster.

Brent tried to keep her calm. 'Tors, take a deep breath. You need to stay calm. Don't give anything away. Don't act suspiciously.'

'I get that, Brent, but I need to find out if he's gone. If it didn't work, we have to come up with something else, and fast.'

'Let's cross that bridge only if we need to. Go to work now, where you will be safe with the team, and call me as soon as you hear anything.'

Tory nodded as she picked up her handbag and keys. Thank goodness Laura was with her grandparents. She'd have picked up on the tension and asked too many questions.

Thirty minutes later, and half an hour early for work, Tory sat at her desk. Anxious, she watched the door for Carolyn to arrive.

'What's up, Tory? You keep jumping every time the door opens,' Glen, her workmate, asked as he walked past her desk.

'Nothing. I'm waiting for Caro. Need to ask her something.'

'Right. What's she been up to now?'

Tory gave him a mind-your-own-business look before turning to her computer and trying to look busy. She was appalled with herself for acting so suspiciously. Tory thought if anyone was looking for a killer, she may as well put a guilty sign on her forehead. The clock on her computer screen ticked over at an excruciatingly slow pace. Carolyn wasn't late. It was still five minutes before her nine o'clock start time.

When she finally walked in, she nodded in Tory's direction and moved her head a fraction toward the tearoom. Tory slipped out of her seat and followed her. Carolyn went through the pretence of making coffee while Tory checked that no one followed them into the empty tearoom.

'Tell me what happened,' she whispered, her voice strained with urgency. Her heart beat hard.

'I'm not sure,' Carolyn whispered back. 'I slipped the poison into his coffee. He wasn't suspicious. He drank it as I walked out. I sat in my car for twenty minutes to see if an ambulance came, but none did. So, I don't know.'

'This is killing me. How can we find out?'

'We can't risk asking in case it gives us away. In a few days, I guess I could have breakfast at the motel again and enquire discreetly about him, but not till after his Wednesday check-out day.'

'Yes, that would work, I suppose. Still, that's three days away. I'm not sure if I can wait that long.'

'You'll have to. Remember, be careful, Tory. If we didn't hurt him, he will still be coming for you.'

CHAPTER 42

The lift seemed to take forever. He watched the floor numbers above the door, slowly count upwards as the lift edged towards his room level. A wave of nausea swept over Anton as he touched his room card on the keypad. Oh God, he felt awful. His face flushed hot, and his hands felt sweaty.

Anton pushed the door open and headed straight to the bathroom. He rested his hands on the sink and looked at himself in the mirror. Another wave of nausea hit him. He winced and gagged as exhaustion swept over him. He splashed water on his face, then ran his hand along the wall for support as he walked carefully to the bed. His legs were heavy. The room seemed to be pulsing. He eased himself down to sit on the bed, leant forward, and rested his head in his hands. His heart raced. Dizziness hit him. He took deep breaths, trying to still his heart and clear his head.

I am not well. I need help.

His heart pounded so hard he felt it beating in his throat. As he sat up straight, spots swam in front of his eyes.

Shit, what is happening to me? Oh God, I feel awful. I need a doctor.

Anton felt scared. He knew something was terribly wrong.

His heart beat so hard it hurt.

Panicked, Anton reached for the telephone next to the bed. His fingers touched the handpiece, but he couldn't get them to close around the receiver. The spots in his eyes turned suddenly to darkness. As he took his last breath, his chest felt like it was being crushed in a vice, and he groaned in pain. His eyes flew open, unseeing, as he toppled forward onto the floor with a soft thud.

* * *

Tory spent a nervous day going through the motions of work. If he asked, she couldn't tell Frank what she did for the day. Nothing registered in her mind except Anton's fate. Five o'clock eventually arrived, and she and Carolyn left work together.

'Girlfriend, I'll follow you home. Keep your eyes out for Anton.'

At home, Brent's truck was in the garage. He greeted them as they walked through the door.

'Any news?' Brent asked, his face anxious.

Both shook their heads.

'Anton didn't follow us home from work,' Tory told him. 'Maybe that's a good sign?'

'I'll turn on the television in case there is a story on him in the news,' Brent said.

'I'll check on the computer in case something has been posted,' Tory said as she logged on and scouted for local news.

'Nothing about an elderly man dying in the motel,' Tory said. She shook her head and turned to the others.

'You know, if the poison killed him, they might not make a news story about him dying. We wanted them to assume he had a heart attack. If that's what they thought happened, they might keep it quiet. No motel would go to the media to say a guest died in one of the rooms. It wouldn't be good publicity,' Brent said.

'Yes, true. They'd want to keep that quiet,' Tory agreed. 'The media would only run a story if they suspected it was murder.'

'Which means we'll have to rely on gossip,' Carolyn said. 'I can't wait until Wednesday or Thursday. I'll go back to the motel for breakfast tomorrow. If he's there, we'll know it didn't work, and if he's not, I'll see what I can find out.'

CHAPTER 43

12 months later

Sitting on the sidelines, Tory watched Brent leap in the air, take a high mark, twist sideways, and handball the football to Karl as he ran past toward the goals.

'Woo-hoo,' she cheered, her one free arm pumping the air.

It was an early-season game, and the afternoon sun still held warmth. It was a pleasant afternoon to sit and watch the match. Tory gently rocked the pram next to her, and Laura sat on a rug in front of her, playing with her dolls and cheering from time to time when she noticed her daddy near the ball.

'Is Oliver asleep yet?' Carolyn asked, peering into the pram.

'Yes, contented like a newly fed bub should be.' Tory smiled at her.

'You know, you guys look like the perfect family. Two kids, people mover. Probably have room for one more, too,' Carolyn teased.

Just before Oliver was born, the banks finally resolved the credit issues arising from her stolen identity, so Tory and Brent were able to take out a loan to buy a car. Tory returned Nan's car, which now sat back in Caro's garage.

'I think we're pretty happy with the two beautiful babies we have, Caro, but never say never, I suppose. Maybe if you and Karl ever tie the knot, you can have the next bub?'

'We'll see,' Carolyn said with a dreamy smile.

Tory reflected on where they were twelve months ago. Frantic, not knowing if Anton was alive or if they had been successful in poisoning him. Every car driving past and every doorknock signalled a potential visit from the police to arrest them. Later at the motel, Carolyn was able to confirm with Rose that the generous-tipping old man staying with them had, unfortunately, passed away in his room. She revealed the housekeeping staff discovered him late morning.

Every moment, Tory expected a police investigation. They heard nothing. Days passed, then weeks. They could have relaxed if they had known a heart attack in a person in their eighties was not viewed as suspicious and would not trigger an autopsy or police investigation.

Soon after Anton's death, the football season started, and Brent was selected in the team. On the sidelines at the first game of the season, with Brent's parents sitting beside her, Tory thought she would have a heart attack when Detective Blunt showed up at the game. The detective, dressed in jeans and a casual top, walked up to her.

'Hi, Tory. How are you? Beautiful day for it, hey?'

'Er, yes. How are you?' Tory stammered. She almost wet herself in fear, and her palms started to sweat.

'Good. Come to watch my nephew have a kick. He's number twenty-three for the away team,' she said, pointing out a player to Tory.

Relief washed through Tory.

'Well, have a nice day. I'd better go and find his mum to sit with.'

Tory watched the detective walk away, unable to think for a moment. She looked around and saw Gail observing her. Tory's face must've shown the fear and then relief of the moment.

Gail laid her hand on top of Tory's.

'Looks like everything's good,' Gail said. She nodded in the detective's direction. 'You and Brent can get back to normal now.'

Tory looked into Gail's eyes. She was sure Brent's parents weren't aware of what they did to Anton. But Gail, while not coming out and asking, sensed their involvement in something. Tory thought Gail guessed they had taken some sort of serious intervention, but to her credit, she didn't ask what, and Tory appreciated her support. Tory patted Gail's hand and nodded.

'Yes, thankfully, you may be right.'

It was nice to have family around her, family who supported her. Family she could depend on. They made her feel worthy of being loved.

The siren blared, signalling the end of the game. Brent's team won the day, with Brent awarded the best-on-ground trophy. She saw his teammates hoist him onto their shoulders and carry him off the field, cheering. Both Brent's parents clapped wildly and turned to her, smiling. Gordon gave her a hug in his excitement. After the game, they drove home, taking Laura with them while leaving Tory and Brent to celebrate the team's win.

Later, in the clubrooms, Tory told Brent of her earlier experience with the detective.

'It looks like we might be in the clear,' Brent said with relief, drink in hand and wearing a huge grin.

'We might be,' Tory said as she wrapped her arm around him.

They both looked across the room to where Carolyn and Karl stood, deep in conversation.

'Karl is going to have his work cut out for him to hook that woman,' Brent said.

'He may've already succeeded,' Tory replied with a smile.

'He better not piss her off. I know what she is capable of,' whispered Brent into Tory's ear.

'Shhhh,' Tory said and slapped him playfully. 'Caro told me she pulled out all the plants in question and buried them. She doesn't plan to do an encore.'

'Can we trust her?'

'With our lives,' Tory responded as she grabbed Brent's hand and, grinning from ear to ear, led him towards Carolyn and Karl.

ACKNOWLEDGEMENTS

A big thank you to my beta readers, Elizabeth Mitchell, Barry Young, and Alison Madeline. Your insights and advice were invaluable.

Thanks also Kim Sorrenson and Raquel Vogel for answering my long list of questions regarding police matters.

BOOK CLUB QUESTIONS: *RUN TILL YOU CAN'T*

1. Did you like or dislike the characters and why? Did it influence how much you enjoyed the book?

2. What are all of the factors that impact the choices characters in the book have and how they make decisions? Do you think these factors reflect what it's like in the world today? What makes you say that?

3. Did you relate to any of the characters or situations?

4. What was the most memorable or impactful scene/s in the book?

5. How did the author build tension and suspense throughout the story?

6. Did you find the authors style easy to read?

7. The plot was based on potentially true events? How did it compare with your prior knowledge of such event/s? What did you learn?

8. How did you feel about the ending? Was it satisfying or did you want more?